IT'S TIME FOR STORY HOUR

By Elizabeth Hough Sechrist and Janette Woolsey

IT'S TIME TO GIVE A PLAY

NEW PLAYS FOR RED LETTER DAYS

IT'S TIME FOR THANKSGIVING

IT'S TIME FOR CHRISTMAS

IT'S TIME FOR EASTER

IT'S TIME FOR BROTHERHOOD

By Elizabeth Hough Sechrist

POEMS FOR RED LETTER DAYS

ONE THOUSAND POEMS FOR CHILDREN

THIRTEEN GHOSTLY YARNS

HEIGH-HO FOR HALLOWEEN

CHRISTMAS EVERYWHERE

RED LETTER DAYS

IT'S
TIME
for
STORY HOUR

COMPILED BY

*Elizabeth Hough Sechrist
and Janette Woolsey*

Illustrations by Elsie Jane McCorkell

MACRAE SMITH COMPANY · PHILADELPHIA

TO

Mary Leona Huber

AND

Alice, Joanne, Kimberley and Jennifer

J
398
S

10/65

Library of Congress Catalog Card Number 64-23918
Manufactured in the United States of America

6411

Acknowledgments

The editors wish to express their thanks and appreciation to the following authors and publishers for their kind permission to include their stories in this volume:

Mr. Henry Beston for "Seller of Dreams," from *Firelight Fairy Book* by Henry Beston, published by Little, Brown & Company. Mr. Francesco M. Bianco for "The Baker's Daughter," from *A Street of Little Shops* by Margery Williams Bianco, published by Doubleday & Company, Inc., 1932. Doubleday & Company, Inc. for "The Bean Boy," from *California Fairy Tales* by Monica Shannon; copyright 1926 by Doubleday & Company, Inc.; reprinted by permission of the publisher. E. P. Dutton & Co., Inc. for "Cheese, Peas and Chocolate Pudding" by Betty Van Witsen from the book *Believe and Make-believe* edited by Lucy Sprague Mitchell and Irma Simonton Black, copyright © 1956 by The Bank Street College of Education, reprinted by permission of E. P. Dutton & Co., Inc.; and for "The Baker's New Coat" from the book *Chitter Chat Stories* by Margaret Cabell Self, copyright 1946 by E. P. Dutton & Co., Inc., reprinted by permission of the publisher. Harcourt, Brace & World, Inc. for "The Fox and the Bear" from *The Magic Listening Cap*, copyright 1955 by Hoshiko Uchida, reprinted by permission of Harcourt, Brace & World, Inc.; for "The Shepherd's Nosegay" from *The Shepherd's Nosegay*, copyright 1920 by Parker Fillmore, renewed 1948 by Louise Fillmore, reprinted by permission of Harcourt, Brace & World, Inc.; and for "The White Horse Girl and the Blue Wind Boy" from *Rootabaga Stories* by Carl Sandburg, copyright 1922, 1923 by Harcourt, Brace & World, Inc., renewed 1950, 1951 by Carl Sandburg, reprinted by permission of the publishers. Harper & Row, Publishers, Incorporated, for "The Man Whose Trade Was Tricks" from *Yes and No Stories* by George and Helen Papashvily, copyright 1946 by George and Helen Waite Papashvily, reprinted with the permission of Harper & Row, Publishers, Incorporated; and for "How Boots Befooled the King" from *The Wonder Clock* by Howard Pyle, and "Farmer Griggs's Boggart" from *Pepper and Salt by* Howard Pyle, both published by Harper & Row, Publishers, Incorporated. Houghton Mifflin Company for "The Cat and the Parrot" from *How to Tell Stories to Children* by Sara Cone Bryant, and for "The Little Jackal and the Alligator" and "How Brother Rabbit Fooled the Whale and the Elephant" from *Stories to Tell to Children* by Sara Cone Bryant, both published by Houghton Mifflin Company. J. B. Lippincott Company for "The Sack of Truth" from *Picture Tales from Spain* by Ruth Sawyer, copyright 1936 by J. B. Lippincott Company, published by J. B. Lippincott Company; for "The King's Rijstepap" and "The Magic Cap" from *Picture Tales from Holland* by Johan Hart;

for "The Golden Boat" from *Picture Tales from the Chinese* by Berta Metzger; for "Rags and Tatters" and "Companions of the Forest" from *The Italian Fairy Book* by Anne MacDonnell; and for "Twigmuntus, Cowbelliantus, Perchnosius" and "The Old Woman and the Tramp" from *Swedish Fairy Tales* by G. Djurklo, all published by J. B. Lippincott Company. Macrae Smith Company for "Benito the Faithful" from *Once in the First Times* by Elizabeth Hough Sechrist, published by Macrae Smith Company, copyright 1949. McGraw-Hill Book Company, Inc. for "The Gods Know," with permission of McGraw-Hill Book Co., Inc./Whittlesey House, from *Legends of the United Nations* by Frances Frost, copyright © 1943 by Frances Frost. Thomas Nelson & Sons for *Down, Down the Mountain* by Ellis Credle, Thomas Nelson & Sons, 1934, 1962. Cox, Treanor, Shaughnessy & Graham, Counsellors at Law, and the Estate of Frances Jenkins Olcott for "The Most Magnificent Cook of All" from *Wonder Tales from Windmill Lands,* and for "The Magic Dumplings" from *Wonder Tales from China Seas,* both by Frances Jenkins Olcott. G. P. Putnam's Sons for "The Strange Visitor," "Tom Tit Tot," "Lazy Jack" and "The Three Sillies" from *English Fairy Tales* by Joseph Jacobs; and for "The Three Wishes," from *More English Fairy Tales,* by Joseph Jacobs, published by G. P. Putnam's Sons. Mrs. Frances G. Wickes for "The Conjure Wives" by Frances G. Wickes.

Preface

"Once upon a time . . ." These are the magic words that transport boys and girls to another world peopled with princes and princesses, fairies and giants, ogres, dragons and animals that talk. The bridge between their everyday world and the land of make-believe is happily crossed through the art of a skillful storyteller.

Storytellers turn to many sources for their material. The world's folk literature provides a treasure house of almost unlimited resources. More than half the stories in this book are traditional. Supplementing them are stories from creative writers of a more modern period. They range from Howard Pyle's humorous "Farmer Grigg's Boggart" to Carl Sandburg's poetic "The White Horse Girl and the Blue Wind Boy."

The storyteller making his choice will be influenced by such factors as (1) the age range of the children in the audience; (2) the size of the audience; whether it is a small, intimate group or a large roomful; (3) the special event for which the story is chosen; (4) the type of story in which the storyteller excels.

Many other anthologies have been compiled for the aid of the storyteller. Some are general in nature, while others have been planned around specific subjects. In selecting the stories for this anthology, we have tried first of all to bring together the ones which in our own experience as storytellers have been favorites with the children. Some are funny, some are romantic, and others tell of strange and weird happenings. All of our forty stories have one quality in common: they have been good stories to tell.

We hope our collection will be useful to storytellers and—equally important—will be enjoyable to boys and girls who like a good story to read.

ELIZABETH HOUGH SECHRIST and JANETTE WOOLSEY

Contents

≺ *Part One*

SOME NEW FAVORITES

Down Down the Mountain

In a little log cabin away up in the Blue Ridge Mountains there lived a little girl named Hetty and her brother Hank.

Although their home was a small one, it was a cozy place to live. There was a big stone fireplace at one end. That was where Mammy cooked beans and cornmeal mush and fried pork in a big, black frying pan.

There was a big bed in one corner and a little bed in the other corner, and in the middle of the room there was a long table made of planks. That was where Mammy and Pappy and Hetty and Hank ate their dinner every day.

All kinds of things hung from the rafters: strings of shucky beans, bunches of bright red peppers, ears of popcorn all tied together, hams, and sausages, and baskets full of this and that.

Never in all their lives had Hetty or Hank had a pair of shoes. In the summer it was fun to run around barefoot, but when winter came, and the snow lay on the mountains like a chilly white blanket, their little feet were blue with cold and they longed for a pair of shoes.

They each wanted a beautiful shining pair that sang, "Creaky-squeaky-creaky-squeaky," every time they walked.

They begged their mammy to buy them some shoes, but she said, "You can't find shoes like that in these hills! Such shining shoes come from the town, away down down at the foot of the mountain."

So they asked their pappy, but he said, "There's not a cent of money in this household. We've everything we need right here in these hills."

Hetty and Hank felt very sad, but they did not give up.

"Let's ask our granny," said Hetty. And they did.

"Some shining shoes?" chirped Granny. "I'll tell you how you can get them yourselves."

"How? How?" cried Hetty and Hank.

"Plant some turnip seeds," said Granny, "and when they have grown into fine big turnips, you can trade them off for some shining, creaky, squeaky shoes."

"Thanky, ma'am, that's what we'll do," cried Hetty and Hank.

They raced away and planted some turnip seeds in a tilled field right next to Pappy's corn patch.

Home they went singing,

> *Our fields are high up in the air,*
> *We wouldn't dare plant pumpkins there,*
> *For pumpkins grow so big and round,*
> *They'd break right off and tumble down.*
> *But turnips grow on hills or vales,*
> *Because they twist their little tails*
> *Around the rocks and hold on tight*
> *And don't let go for day or night!*

When Hetty and Hank got home it was dark. The whippoor-wills were calling sadly from the deep woods, "Whip-poor-will! Whip-poor-will!" and a little owl was asking, "Who? Who-o-o?"

Mammy was waiting for them. She gave them a nice supper of corn bread and butter and yellow honey. Then she tucked them snugly into bed. They dreamed all night about shining shoes that played a creaky, squeaky tune, just like Pappy's fiddle.

The next day they climbed up the steep, steep mountainside to see if the turnip seeds had come up. But they had not, and Hetty and Hank had to wait and wait and wait, before they spied the baby turnip leaves peeping out of the ground.

Then there was plenty of work for Hetty and Hank! They had to clear away the weeds each day, and chase away the worms and the bugs and the grasshoppers that came for a taste of nice green turnip leaves.

When there was no rain and the little turnips felt dry and thirsty, Hetty and Hank had to bring big buckets of water to make them fresh and green again.

The little turnips were very grateful. They grew and grew until they were the finest and the biggest turnips to be found anywhere in the hill country.

Then Hetty and Hank brought Granny and Mammy and Pappy up to see them.

"Sakes alive!" cried Mammy, "I never saw such big turnips!"

"Yes, sirree!" smiled Granny. "These are mighty juicy turnips."

"And they'll fetch a fine price in the town," said Pappy. "Hetty and Hank shall have the old gray horse to take them down the mountain."

So Hank quickly brought the gray horse. Then they pulled up all the beautiful turnips and packed them into a big bag.

Pappy laid the bag proudly across the gray horse's back, then he gave Hetty and Hank a boost and settled them safely right in front of the turnips. Now they were ready to go.

"We'll keep to the road," promised Hetty and Hank. Hank pulled on the reins. Hetty gave the gray horse a slap on the side, and they were off.

"Good-by!" cried Granny and Mammy and Pappy.

"Good-by!" waved Hetty and Hank. And away they went, clippity, cloppity, down the road to town.

They had not gone very far before they came to an old man cutting sugar cane in a field beside the road.

"Howdy, young ones!" he called. "What have you in that big bag?"

"Some turnips we're taking to sell in the town," said Hank proudly.

"Oh, my! Turnips!" cried the old man. "How I'd love some nice, juicy turnips for my dinner! Couldn't you spare me just a few?"

"I suppose we wouldn't miss just a few," said Hetty, and she gave him some.

On they jogged between great bushes of pink mountain laurel, and after a while they came to an old woman who was making soap in a big black kettle.

"Howdy, children!" she called. "What have you in that big bag?"

"Some turnips we're taking down to town," said Hank.

"Turnips!" cried the old woman. "Mercy me! How I'd love just a taste of turnip for my dinner! Couldn't you spare me just two, one for my old man and one for me?"

"I suppose we wouldn't miss just two," said Hetty, and she gave her two big ones.

Down, down, down they went between the rows of tall blue mountains, down, down, down until they came to a little stream flowing over the rocks. There the little road ended. They looked here, they looked there, they looked everywhere, but it was nowhere to be seen.

But just then along came a woman on horseback, splishing and splashing right down the middle of the stream.

"What's the matter, young ones?" she called.

"We've lost the little road to town," said Hank.

"Follow the creek," said the woman. "That's all the road there is in these parts."

So Hetty and Hank went splashing along and along and pretty soon they spied the little road leading up from the water.

They said good-by to the kind woman and gave her a bunch of turnips for her dinner.

On they went along the little road beneath the tall pine trees. After a while they overtook a man who was driving a flock of turkeys down to town. "Howdy," said the man. "What have you in that bag?"

"Some turnips we're taking to sell in the town," said Hank.

"Oh my stars!" said the man. "Turnips! and I've had nary a bit to eat since break of dawn. A nice, juicy turnip would taste mighty good now, for I've been running after these turkeys 'til I'm nigh worn out."

"We'll have to give him a handful of turnips," said Hetty. And she did.

"Thanky, thanky," said the man. "You're kind and generous young ones!"

Now they were very near to town. They could look down and see the roof tops in the valley.

The little road became so smooth and straight that the gray horse broke into a gallop.

"Here's the town!" cried Hank.

Along they went, clippity clop, clippity clop, past the schoolhouse, past the church, past the courthouse, and suddenly there was the little red store.

"Whoa!" cried Hank, pulling on the reins. "Here's the place to trade our turnips off for some shining shoes!"

They climbed down and lifted off the sack. Somehow it felt very light and very, very empty. Had they given all their turnips away?

Hetty put her hand into the bag and brought out one large, fat, lonesome turnip. It was the only one left.

And there—shining through the store window—were those beautiful, creaky, squeaky, shining shoes!

Hetty and Hank gazed at them longingly. But one turnip would not buy a pair of shoes.

Two big tears began to roll down Hetty's cheeks.

"There! There!" said Hank. "No use crying. We'll just walk around and see the sights. Come on."

So they walked along the little road looking this way and that way. They saw the big covered wagons, all loaded with apples, come rumbling down from the hills. They saw the men trading horses in the courthouse square. Then a train went thundering past and they watched it with round eyes.

Along and along they went and after a while they came to a field where there were many, many people. A big sign over the gate said

COUNTY FAIR

Hetty and Hank went hustling and bustling about in the crowd. Pretty soon they came to a long row of tables, each one groaning with a different kind of vegetable. There were tomatoes on this one, and beans on that one, and pumpkins on the other one.

"Oh, here are some turnips!" cried Hetty.

"Are they as big as ours?" asked Hank.

Hetty held up her turnip. It seemed larger and juicier than the rest.

"Howdy, young ones," said the old man who was looking at the turnips. "Do you want to enter that turnip in the contest?"

"What contest?" asked Hank.

"Why there's a prize offered for the finest turnip at the fair," replied the old man.

"Mercy me!" said Hetty. "Let's try it."

"You bet your life!" said Hank.

So the old man wrote their names on a tag and tied it to the fat turnip. Then he laid it carefully among all the other turnips.

"You are just in the nick of time," he said, "for I was just getting ready to do the judging."

He began to examine the turnips. He weighed each one to see how heavy it was. He felt each one to see how firm it was. And when he had tried them all he held one large turnip high above his head.

"Folks!" he cried. "Here's the finest turnip at the fair. It belongs to a little girl and a little boy!"

Hetty and Hank listened with all their ears.

"Come forward, young ones, and receive the prize!"

Hetty held out her hand, and there looking up at her was a crisp ten dollar bill.

"Oh thank you sir!" cried Hetty and Hank. "Now we can buy our shining shoes!"

They dashed along past the beans and tomatoes. They ran past the squash and skipped past the potatoes. They dodged

through the hustle and the bustle on the fair grounds. They raced along the street until they came to the little red store.

The storekeeper was standing behind the counter.

"We want to buy some beautiful, creaky, squeaky shoes!" said Hank, all out of breath.

The storekeeper got down his brightest shoes, and Hetty and Hank each chose a pair that played a creaky, squeaky tune.

Then they bought some gifts to take home with them. A yellow hat for Pappy, a bright sash for Mammy and a big, red handkerchief and a package of needles for Granny.

And off they started on the long trip home. Up, up, up they wound, round and round the mountain, past the pink laurel flowers, along the little stream and underneath the tall pine trees.

After a long, long climb they reached their own little cabin. There sat Mammy and Pappy and Granny waiting on the porch. How pleased they were to see Hetty and Hank and all the new things they had brought!

The next day was Sunday, so they put on their beautiful things and went to preaching.

Hetty and Hank walked proudly into the meetinghouse. Their shoes were playing such a creaky, squeaky tune that all the people craned their necks to see who could be wearing such beautiful shoes.

ELLIS CREDLE

The Gods Know

In the temple court the Sacred Horse was in a temper. He glared at a thin-faced, ragged little girl who was peering through the bars at him. "That rascal of an attendant has been stealing my bean cake again!" he said furiously. "And I am the Sacred Horse! I don't know what my life is coming to!"

The little girl held a dirty small hand through the bars. "You may have my bread, and perhaps it will keep you from being so hungry."

The Sacred Horse rolled his eyes suspiciously at the very small piece of coarse pone she held out; then he accepted it, and it tasted quite good. Her dark eyes smiled at him. "Well, who are you?" he asked crossly, without even saying thank you.

"I don't know," she answered gravely. "I think I fell from the moon."

The Horse couldn't help laughing. "But who takes care of you?"

"I do."

"How old are you?"

"Nine. I sleep anywhere, in the fields or under the trees or in the temple if it rains. And I get so lonely sometimes, I wish I were dead."

When he saw the tears in her soft eyes, the Sacred Horse swallowed and blinked, himself, and said hastily, "There, my child, don't cry. I've just been thinking how differently you and I feel about this freedom you have. I've been shut up in this temple for fifteen years, and I would love to roam about from place to place and sleep in the fields and under the trees as you do."

The little girl scrubbed her eyes with a grimy fist and stared at him in astonishment. "You would?"

"I certainly would. Here I am imprisoned in this temple court for fools to gaze at, believing that I am sacred."

"But aren't you?"

The Horse shook his head. "Not half as much as you, my dear, who gave me your crust of bread."

"I should think you'd like it," she protested, "having people worship you and offer up their incense in your name."

"Well, I don't," said the Horse emphatically. "I'll admit that my head was turned when I was a young colt, and I was very conceited for a while at the sight of people coming to offer me their prayers and bowing down before me. But I soon outgrew that."

The child nodded wisely. "There isn't much sense in vanity."

The Horse suppressed a smile. "No, there isn't." He sighed. "And then I grew impatient of being a prisoner. I tried twice to get away, but my jailers caught me. Then I refused to eat and meant to starve myself to death, but after I was good and hungry, that seemed pretty silly. And now this scoundrel has taken to robbing me of my bean cake. I could kick!" said the Sacred Horse fiercely.

"You still have much more to eat than we poor people. I'd be happy to get in three days what they give you at one feeding."

"Hmm," said the Horse thoughtfully. "You would? Then I'll tell you what let's do—let's change places!"

"What?"

"Oh, I don't mean that you change into a horse and I into a girl," he said, chuckling. "That would be rather impossible. But if you'll come here tonight and let me out, then you may come in and take my place. I'll have the freedom I want so much, and you'll have fun being worshiped and fed by the people."

The little girl was breathless. "But won't they kill me for letting you loose and pretending that I'm sacred?"

"I told you," said the Horse, a trifle exasperated, "you're just as sacred as I am. And they'll simply call it another wonder of the gods when they see you instead of me."

"When do you wish me to come?" she asked, her eyes shining.

"At midnight," said the Horse happily. "Then I can get far beyond Lan T'an before dawn, where people won't know I am the Sacred Horse. Then I shall set out on my adventures."

That night after the moon had risen, and midnight ap-

proached, the little girl hurried to the temple and found the stall of the Sacred Horse.

The Horse was watching for her anxiously. "I was afraid you wouldn't come."

"I promised to come. But what shall I say if the priests and the people ask me any questions?"

The Horse replied, "Say simply, 'The gods know.' Then be silent and look wise. They will be sure that their Sacred Horse has been changed into a goddess. Here is a chest of beautiful silken cloths which are my trappings for state occasions. Drape them around yourself so that your ragged things will not show."

"You are so kind and thoughtful." The little girl drew back the bars and set the Horse free. "Wherever you go, remember you have one friend who will always think of you. And come back if you should grow tired, and I shall comfort you." And she stroked the Horse's neck gently, as high up as she could reach.

He nuzzled her thin cheek in farewell and trotted out through the gateway of the temple court. The child closed the bars of the sacred stall. She wrapped the silken cloths about herself and lay down to sleep, thinking fondly of the Sacred Horse and wishing him happiness on his travels.

A little later she awoke with a start and heard two hoarse voices talking outside the bars of the sacred stall.

"What's a Sacred Horse?" said one roughly. "If he can gallop, that's all we care. This treasure of the Mandarin's is heavy. Sling it on this old nag and we'll get out of this valley before we're captured."

"But what'll happen to us if we get caught on the Sacred Horse?"

"Don't be a coward at this point!" said the first voice angrily. "The Horse can't tell on us, and a little race through the country won't hurt him any." The thief coughed. "Come on, let's get started. Who'll know about it anyhow?"

"The gods know," said a clear, sweet voice.

Terror-stricken, the thieves turned and saw a tiny form clad in heavenly raiment and a small fair face with dark eyes that looked into their very souls. They cried out in fear, dropped their plunder and fled into the night.

The little girl laughed gaily at the rumpus she had caused. She opened the bars and pulled and tugged until she had dragged in the heavy bag of the Mandarin's treasure. She opened the bag and spread in the moonlight the silver and golden ornaments, the jade, the precious ivory, and gazed in astonishment at beauty such as she had never dreamed of in her short life. She curled up in the moonlight, feasting her eyes upon these wonders, until once more she fell asleep.

When she awoke, the sun was halfway up the sky and the court was filled with staring people. And in front of the crowd stood the Mandarin himself, in all his glittering clothes, gazing at the marvel of a child where the Sacred Horse should be. He looked from her to his stolen treasure spread out on the ground, and asked in an awed tone, "Where did you come from, my child?"

"The gods know," she answered gravely.

"But where is the Sacred Horse?"

"The gods know," she replied once more.

The Mandarin's guard of soldiers grew pale, and many of the people fell on their knees, murmuring, "A goddess! She is a goddess!"

The Mandarin waved his jeweled hand toward his treasure. "These were stolen from my palace last night. How did they come here?"

"The gods know," she said again, looking full into his eyes.

"Truly the gods know all," the Mandarin cried, "and this is a miracle they have wrought." And at once he and his followers sank to their knees and pressed their foreheads to the earth before the little girl in the stall of the Sacred Horse.

The people hailed her as the little Goddess of the Bereft and came to pray to her that what had been stolen from them and what they had lost might be returned. They built a great palace for her and came every day to worship her. But the little girl did not forget the Horse and wished that he were there to share her splendor, although she hoped that he was having a fine time adventuring in freedom about the world.

So ten years passed and the little girl grew to womanhood; yet for all her riches and the reverence given her by men, she was lonely and unhappy, for she had no friend.

One night as she was strolling alone about her moonlit inner garden, a servant came to her and kowtowed. "Most gracious goddess," he said, "a strange thing has been happening at the outer gate. An hour ago there was a rattling at the gate, and when the porter opened it he found an old white horse, riderless, trying to enter. He drove the horse away, but the knocking began again. The more he beats it, the more the horse comes back."

"Let the horse enter," said the girl. "Not even an animal shall be denied an audience."

When the servant returned, he led by the mane an old white horse with drooping head and faltering pace. The girl dismissed the servant and turned to the weary horse.

"Sacred Horse, you have come back!" she cried. "And to you I owe all this homage and splendor!"

"Yes, I have returned," he answered in a disheartened voice. "I have come to beg of you a corner of your stables, where I may die near the one mistress whom I adore."

She gazed at him with pity. "But did you not enjoy the freedom you desired so much?"

"No," he said, gazing at her sadly, "for liberty is nothing without friendship, and friendship is nothing without love. When I ruled in the temple, I was master of men, for they believed me sacred; but in the world where I was free, every man became master. And in neither life did I have friendship. You alone as a little girl were my friend; and now I have returned to ask your protection and to die."

The girl threw her arms about the neck of the Horse and once more stroked him; she laid her head against his neck while tears of compassion fell from her dark eyes.

"Is it possible," asked the Horse hesitantly, "that you, too, are unhappy?"

"The gods know," she answered.

As she spoke, her being was pierced with a wondrous thrill, and lifting her head, she saw that the Horse had vanished and that her arms were about the neck of a young and handsome prince.

"Oh, my beloved," he murmured, holding her close in his arms, "did I not say that liberty is nothing without friendship, and friendship nothing without love?"

"The gods know," she repeated.

"Yes," he said, in a voice shaken with profound and holy passion, "the gods know!"

FRANCES FROST

The Baker's Daughter

O but the Baker's Daughter is beautiful!

The Baker's Daughter has yellow hair, and every night it is curled with rags, and every morning it stands out in a frizzy fluff round her head. The Baker's Daughter has blue dresses and pink dresses and spotted dresses, with flounces and flounces on them; she has beads around her neck and jingly bracelets and a ring with a real stone. All the girls in class sigh with envy of the Baker's Daughter.

But the Baker's Daughter is proud. She points her chin and she turns up her nose, and she is very, very superior. You never see her in the Baker's shop. She strolls up and down the sidewalk, sucking her beads.

You all know the Baker's shop, two steps down. It is warm in there, and busy. It smells of hot bread, and every few minutes the Baker, a hot, untidy little man in shirt sleeves, comes up from the basement carrying a big tray of crullers, or shiny rolls, or twisted currant buns. The Baker works hard all day and he never has time to do more than just poke his nose outside the doorway, every hour or so, for a sniff of cool air. It is hard to believe that anything so beautiful as the Baker's Daughter could ever come out of the Baker's shop!

Once I started to write a poem. It began:

> *O it is the Baker's Daughter,*
> *And she is grown so fair, so fair . . .*

I thought I would make a very splendid valentine of it, all written out in a fine hand, with pink roses around and lots of crinkly paper lace, and send it to her, secretly. But unfortunately

I found out that it was too much like a poem that someone else wrote a long time ago, and so I have never finished it. But still it always comes into my mind whenever I see the Baker's Daughter sucking her beads.

There was only one thing in the Baker's shop that at all came up in magnificence to the Baker's Daughter herself, and that was the big round cake that sat in the place of honor, right in the

middle of the Baker's window. It was a chocolate cake, with all sorts of twirls and twiddles of lovely icing on it, and the word BIRTHDAY written in pink sugar letters. For some reason or other the Baker would never sell that cake. Perhaps he was afraid he would never be able to make another one quite so beautiful. He would sell you any other cake from his window but that one, and even if you went there very early of a Friday morning, which is cruller day, when there are no cakes at all, and asked him for a nice party cake, he would say:

"I can let you have one by three o'clock!"

And if you then asked: "But how about the cake in the window?" he would reply:

"That's not for sale. You can have one by three o'clock!"

For though you should offer him dollars and dollars, he would never sell that cake!

I seldom dare to speak to the Baker's Daughter. I am much too humble. But still she has friends. Never little boys; these she points her chin at, from across the street. But there are little girls with whom she is on friendly terms for as much as a week at a time. Naturally they are very proud. If you can't be a princess or a movie star, perhaps the next best thing is to be seen walking up to the drugstore soda fountain with the Baker's Daughter and sitting there beside her on a tall stool eating pineapple sundae.

Now there was one little girl with whom the Baker's Daughter condescended at one time to be friends. Perhaps her name had something to do with it. She was called Carmelita Miggs, and Carmelita is a very romantic and superior name. She had black hair and a pair of bronze slippers, and she was the only little girl ever seen to stroll publicly with the Baker's Daughter, arm in arm. What they talked about no one knew. But Carmelita sometimes wore the Baker's Daughter's beads, and the Baker's Daughter would wear Carmelita's beads, and altogether they were very, very special friends while it lasted.

And it lasted until Carmelita had a birthday party.

The Baker's Daughter of course was invited, and several other of Carmelita's school friends. It was to be a real party, at four in the afternoon, with ice cream. And the Baker's Daughter said, very grandly, that she would bring a cake.

"I will bake you a nice one," said her father, "with orange icing on it. Now let me see . . . how many of you will there be?"

But that wasn't at all what the Baker's Daughter wanted. Anyone at all could bring a cake with orange icing. "I will choose my own cake!" thought the Baker's Daughter.

But all she said was, "That will be very nice!"

And in the afternoon, while her father was down in the bake-shop kitchen putting the last twiddle on the orange cake (for he wanted to make it something very special), and while her mother was taking forty winks in the back parlor, and the bakery cat was sound asleep, with her four paws curled under her, behind the counter, the Baker's Daughter crept into the shop on tiptoe, in all her finery, and stole—yes, *stole*—that big, magnificent cake from the very middle of the shop window!

You see, she had had her eye on it, all along!

She lifted it up—and a nice, light cake it seemed—wooden platter and all, and she covered it over with sheets of waxy paper and carried it round to Carmelita's house.

O but she looked proud, walking down the street with that big cake in her arms! Everyone turned to look at her.

"What a lovely cake!" cried all the little boys and girls when she arrived at Carmelita's house.

And the wrappings were taken off very carefully, and it was set right in the middle of the table, with candles all around it.

"*What* a nice light cake!" said Carmelita's mother.

"All good cakes are light!" said the Baker's Daughter.

"It was very, very kind of your father to make such a splendid cake," said Carmelita's mother.

"I chose it myself!" said the Baker's Daughter, tossing her head.

They talked a little, very politely, and Carmelita Miggs showed all her birthday presents. And at last came the moment for the ice cream to be handed round on little glass plates.

"And now," said Carmelita's mother, "we'll all have some of that delicious cake!"

Carmelita had to cut it, because it was her birthday. She stood there feeling very shy, for there was a great silence all round; everyone's eyes were fixed on the cake, and all one could hear was Tommy Bates busily sucking his ice cream spoon, so as to get through first.

Only the Baker's Daughter sat there proudly, with her skirts spread out, looking indifferent, as though cakes like this were quite an everyday affair with her!

Carmelita took the knife and stuck it into the very middle of the pink icing, and pushed. You could have heard a pin drop.

But the knife didn't go in. Carmelita turned very red, and took a long breath and tried again.

Still the knife wouldn't go in.

"You must try harder, dear," said Carmelita's mother, smiling pleasantly. "I expect the top icing is a little bit stiff! Do you want me to help you?"

Now Carmelita knew that she had been pushing just as hard as she could. It came upon her, all at once, that there must be something very, very queer about that cake! But she took another long breath, again, and this time her mother put *her* hand on the knife, too.

You could have heard *two* pins drop!

And then, suddenly, there was a funny "plop," and the knife went in. And as it went in the cake slipped and turned a sort of somersault, and there it was, upside down, sticking on the tip of the knife that Carmelita's mother was still holding, and everyone looking most surprised. And that wasn't the worst of it!

It was all hollow inside!

In fact, it was just a big pasteboard shell covered over with icing, and *that* was why the Baker would never sell it to anyone!

Can you imagine how the party felt? How the little boys and girls whispered and giggled, how Carmelita wept and the Baker's Daughter grew redder and redder, and snifflier and snifflier, and how Carmelita's mother tried to smooth everything over and pretend that it was really all very funny, and quite the nicest thing that could happen at any birthday party? And how, at the very last minute, while the ice cream was all melting away, they had to send out and buy a real cake, *somewhere else!*

But Carmelita Miggs didn't think it was a joke. She never, never forgave the Baker's Daughter for spoiling her party. For quite a long time she wouldn't speak to her at all. As for the other boys and girls, whenever they met Carmelita or the Baker's Daughter they would say, "Now we'll all have some cake!"

You would think, after this, that the Baker's Daughter would have changed her ways. But not a bit of it! I saw her, only the other day, strolling up and down the sidewalk and sucking her beads just as proud as ever.

As I went past her I whispered very softly, "Now we'll all have some cake!"

And do you know what the Baker's Daughter did? I hate to tell you.

She stuck—out—her—her—tongue!

There, in the middle of the Baker's window, is another cake. This time it has green icing and pink roses, and two little sugar doves on top. It is even grander than the old one, and will probably last twice as long.

Unless, of course, someone else should have a birthday party!

MARGERY WILLIAMS BIANCO

The Seller of Dreams

Once upon a time a mother called her only son into the kitchen, gave him a basket of fine, fresh eggs, and bade him carry them to his Aunt Jane, who lived a few miles down the valley. The son, a lively lad about twelve years of age, obeyed his mother with joy, and clapping his little green hat on his head, stepped forth into the road. It was a beautiful clear morning in the spring, and the earth, released from the icy chains of winter, was rejoicing in her freedom and the return of the sun. A few birds, just back from the southland, rocked on twigs swollen with bursting buds, a thousand rills flowing from everywhere and in every direction sparkled and sang, and the air was sweet with the odor of ploughed fields.

The boy, whose name was Peter, walked along whistling. Suddenly he saw a spot on the road shining as dazzlingly as if a bit of the sun itself had fallen to the earth. "A bit of glass," thought Peter. But it was not a bit of glass after all, but a fine golden florin, which must have dropped from somebody's purse.

Peter stooped, picked up the gold piece, put it in his pocket, and walked off whistling louder than ever. In a little while he came to a place where the road wound down a little hill, and Peter saw, trudging up this hill, a very strange-looking old man. He was a very old man; his face was puckered up into a thousand wrinkles like the skin of a shrunken apple, and he had long, snow-white hair and a white beard that reached almost to his waist. Moreover, he was strangely dressed in a robe of cherry scarlet and wore golden shoes. From a kind of belt hung two horns on silver chains, one an ordinary cow's horn, the other a beautiful horn carved of the whitest ivory and decorated with little figures of men and animals.

"Dreams to sell! Dreams to sell!" called out the old man as soon as he caught sight of Peter. "Don't you want to buy a dream, young man?"

"What kind of dreams have you?" asked Peter.

"Good, bad, true, false—all kinds," replied the seller of dreams. "I have even a few thrilling nightmares. Dreams to sell! Dreams to sell !"

"How much does a dream cost?" asked Peter.

"A golden florin," answered the merchant.

"I'll have one, please," said Peter; and he handed over the florin he had found.

The old man took a kind of wonderful sugarplum out of the ivory horn, and gave it to Peter to eat.

"You will have the dream next time you sleep," said he, and trudged on.

So Peter continued his journey, stopping every once in a while to look back at the strange old man, who was slowly climbing the hill. At length Peter came to a little quiet grove of pines, and there he sat down on a big stone and ate the luncheon which his mother had prepared for him. The sun was high in the heavens; it was close on to high noon. Now, as Peter was contentedly munching his bread and cheese, he heard, at first far away, then quite near at hand, the clear notes of a coachman's horn. The notes of the second call died away in a great pattering of hoofs and tinkling of little bells, and suddenly, arriving in a great swirl of yellow dust, came a magnificent coach drawn by twelve white horses. A lady, very richly dressed and wearing many sparkling diamonds, sat within the coach. To Peter's astonishment, the lady was his Aunt Jane.

The coach stopped with a great jingling of the twelve harnesses, and Aunt Jane leaned out of the window, and said to Peter, "What are you doing here, child?"

"I was on my way to your cottage with a basket of fine fresh eggs," answered Peter.

"Well, it's fortunate I found you," said Aunt Jane, "for I have given up living in the cottage, and have now got a castle of my own. Jump in, Peter, and don't forget your basket."

So Peter climbed into the coach, closed the door behind him, and was driven away. The coach went over hill and down dale; it went through strange forests from whose branches green parrots whooped and shrieked; it rolled through valleys in strange, shin-

ing mountains. Peter stole a look at Aunt Jane and saw that she was wearing a crown.

"Are you a queen, Aunt Jane?" he asked.

"Indeed, I am," replied his aunt. "You see, Peter, two days ago, while I was looking for my white cow who had strayed away, I came upon the magnificent castle to which we are now going. It has four beautiful towers and a door set with diamonds.

" 'Whose castle is this?' I said to the lodgekeeper.

" 'It's nobody's, marm,' said he.

" 'What,' said I; 'do you mean to say that nobody owns this fine castle?'

" 'That's just what I mean to say, marm,' answered he; 'the castle belongs to anyone who wants it.'

"So into the castle I walked, and I didn't go out, you may be sure, till I had been into every room that I could find. Then I put on these clothes and these diamonds, which I found in a cupboard, and went down and told the servants I intended to be queen. You see, Peter dear, there's nothing that a woman of determination and energy can't accomplish."

The coach rolled on, and soon Peter caught sight of Aunt Jane's castle. It was rather large, and had an enormous round tower at each corner—a thing which brought to Peter's mind the picture of an elephant lying on its back. Peter and Aunt Jane, accompanied by a train of servants dressed in blue-and-buff livery, walked into the castle through the diamond-studded door.

"Do you think you could eat a little more of something?" said Aunt Jane, taking off her white kid gloves; "because if you can I'll have a place set for you at the luncheon table."

And Peter, who like all boys, could eat a little more anywhere and at any time, readily answered, "Yes."

So Peter and Aunt Jane sat down to a wonderful little table covered with a snow-white cloth.

"Draw your chair nearer, Peter dear," said Aunt Jane.

"I can't," said Peter. "It's stuck to the floor."

And so it was; the chair was stuck to the floor, and no amount of pushing or pulling could budge it.

"That's odd," said Aunt Jane; "but never mind. I'll push the table over to the chair."

But like the chair, the table refused to budge. Peter then tried to slide his plate of soup closer to him, but the plate, which the servant had placed on the cloth but an instant before, had evidently frozen to the table in some extraordinary manner and could not be moved an inch. The soup in the plate, however, was not fastened to the dish, nor were the wonderful strawberry cakes and the delicious ices with which the dinner closed.

"You don't suppose this castle is enchanted, do you, Aunt Jane?" asked Peter.

"Not a bit of it," replied Aunt Jane. "And even if it were," she continued recklessly, "I shouldn't mind, for there's nothing that a woman of determination and energy can't accomplish." There was a pause, and then Aunt Jane added, "I am going to have some guests to dinner this evening, so run round and amuse yourself as well as you can. There's ever so much to see in the castle, and in the garden there's a pond with swans in it."

Attended by her servants, Aunt Jane majestically walked away. Peter spent the afternoon exploring the castle. He went through room after room; he scurried through the attics like a mouse, and was even lost for a while in the cellars. And everywhere he went, he found everything immovable. The beds, tables, and chairs could neither be moved about nor lifted up, and even the clocks and vases were mysteriously fastened to their places on the shelves.

The night came on. Coach after coach rolled up to the diamond door, which sparkled in the moonlight. When the guests had all arrived, a silver trumpet sounded, and Aunt Jane, dressed in a wonderful gown of flowering brocade edged with pearls, came solemnly down the great stairway of the castle hall. Two little black boys, dressed in oriental costume and wearing turbans, held up her gorgeous train, and she looked very grand indeed. Peter, to his great surprise, found himself dressed in a wonderful suit of plum-colored velvet.

"Welcome, my friends," said Queen Jane, who had opened a wonderful ostrich feather fan. "Are we not fortunate in having so beautiful a night for our dinner?"

And the Queen, giving her arm to a splendid personage in the uniform of an officer of the King's dragoons, led the way to the banquet hall.

The wonderful party, all silks and satins, and gleaming with jewels, swept like a peacock's tail behind her. Soon dinner was over, and the guests began to stray by twos and threes to the ballroom. Aunt Jane and the soldier led off the grand march; then came wonderful, stately minuets, quadrilles, and sweet, old-fashioned waltzes. The merriment was at its height when somebody ran heavily up the great stairs leading to the ballroom, and the guests, turning round to see whence came the clatter, saw standing in the doorway a strange old man dressed in a robe of cherry scarlet and wearing golden shoes. It was the seller of dreams. His white hair was disheveled, his robe was awry, and there was dust on his golden shoes.

"Foolish people!" screamed the old seller of dreams, his voice rising to a shriek. "Run for your lives! This castle lies under a terrible enchantment. In a few minutes it will turn upside down. Have you not seen that everything is fastened to the floor? Run for your lives!"

Immediately there was a great babble of voices, some shrieks, and more confusion, and the guests ran pell-mell down the great stairs and out the castle door. To Peter's dismay, Aunt Jane was not among them. So into the castle he rushed again, calling at the top of his voice, "Aunt Jane! Aunt Jane!" He ran through the brilliantly lit and deserted ballroom; he saw himself running in the great mirrors of the gallery. "Aunt Jane!" he cried; but no Aunt Jane replied.

Peter rushed up the stairs leading to the castle tower, and emerged upon the balcony. He saw the black shadow of the castle thrown upon the grass far below by the full moon; he saw the great forest, so bright above and so dark and mysterious below, and the long, snow-clad range of the Adamant Mountains. Suddenly a voice, louder than the voice of any human being, a voice deep, ringing, and solemn as the sound of a great bell, cried, " 'Tis time!"

Immediately everything became as black as ink, people shrieked, the enchanted castle rolled like a ship at sea, and leaning far to one side, *began to turn upside down*. Peter felt the floor of the balcony tip beneath him; he tried to catch hold of something, but could find nothing; suddenly, with a scream, he fell. He was falling, falling, falling, falling, falling.

When Peter came to himself, instead of its being night, it was still noonday, and he was sitting on the same stone in the same quiet roadside grove from which he had caught sight of his Aunt Jane in her wonderful coach. A blue jay screamed at him from overhead. For Aunt Jane, the coach, and the enchanted castle had been only a dream. Peter, you see, had fallen asleep under the pines, and while he slept, he had dreamed the dream he purchased from the seller of dreams.

Very glad to be still alive, Peter rubbed his eyes, took up his basket of eggs, and went down the road whistling.

HENRY BESTON

Cheese, Peas, and Chocolate Pudding

There was once a little boy who ate cheese, peas, and chocolate pudding. Cheese, peas, and chocolate pudding. Cheese, peas, and chocolate pudding. Every day the same old things: cheese, peas, and chocolate pudding.

For breakfast he would have some cheese. Any kind. Cream cheese, American cheese, Swiss cheese, Dutch cheese, Italian cheese, blue cheese, green cheese, yellow cheese, brick cheese. Even Liederkranz. Just cheese for breakfast.

For lunch he ate peas. Green or yellow peas. Frozen peas, canned peas, dried peas, split peas, black-eyed peas. No potatoes, though—just peas for lunch.

And for supper he would have cheese and peas. And chocolate pudding. Cheese, peas, and chocolate pudding. Cheese, peas, and chocolate pudding. Every day the same old things: cheese, peas, and chocolate pudding.

Once his mother bought a lamb chop for him. She cooked it in a little frying pan on the stove, and she put some salt on it, and gave it to the little boy on a little blue dish. The boy looked at it. He smelled it. (It did smell delicious!) He even touched it. But . . .

"Is this cheese?" he asked.

"It's a lamb chop, darling," said his mother.

The boy shook his head. "Cheese!" he said. So his mother ate the lamb chop herself, and the boy had some cottage cheese.

One day his big brother was chewing a raw carrot. It sounded so good, the little boy reached his hand out for a bite.

"Sure!" said his brother. "Here!" The little boy *almost* put the carrot into his mouth, but at the last minute he remembered, and he said, "Is this peas?"

"No, fella, it's a carrot," said his brother.

"Peas," said the little boy firmly, handing the carrot back.

Once his daddy was eating a big dish of raspberry Jell-O. It looked so shiny red and cool, the little boy came over and held his mouth open.

"Want a taste?" asked his daddy. The little boy looked and

looked at the Jell-O. He almost looked it off the dish. But: "Is it chocolate pudding?" he asked.

"No, son, it's Jell-O," said his daddy.

So the little boy frowned and backed away. "Chocolate pudding!" he said.

His grandma baked cookies for him. "Nope!" said the boy.

His grandpa bought him an ice cream cone. The little boy just shook his head.

His aunt and uncle invited him for a fried-chicken dinner. Everybody ate fried chicken and fried chicken and more fried chicken. Except the little boy. And you know what he ate.

Cheese, peas, and chocolate pudding. Cheese, peas, and chocolate pudding. Every day the same old thing: cheese, peas, and chocolate pudding.

But one day—ah, one day, a very funny thing happened. The little boy was playing puppy. He lay on the floor and growled and barked and rolled over. He crept to the table where his big brother was having lunch.

"Arf-arf!" he barked.

"Good doggie!" said his brother, patting his head. The little boy lay down on his back on the floor and barked again.

But at that minute, his big brother dropped a piece of *something* from his plate. And the little boy's mouth was just ready to say "Arf!" And what do you think happened?

Something dropped into the little boy's mouth. He sat up in surprise. Because *something* was on his tongue. And *something* was warm and juicy and delicious!

And it didn't taste like cheese. And it did *not* taste like peas. And it certainly wasn't chocolate pudding.

The little boy chewed slowly. Each chew tasted better than the last. He swallowed *something* and opened his mouth again. Wide. As wide as he could.

"Want some more?" asked his brother.

The little boy closed his mouth and thought. "That's not cheese," he said.

"No, it's not," said his brother.

"And it isn't peas."

"No, not peas," said his brother.

"And it couldn't be chocolate pudding."

"No, it certainly is not chocolate pudding," smiled his brother. "It's hamburger."

The little boy thought hard. "I like hamburger," he said.

So his big brother shared the rest of his hamburger with the little boy, and ever after that, guess what!

Ever after that, the little boy ate cheese, peas, and chocolate pudding and hamburger.

Until he was your age, of course. When he was your age, he ate everything.

BETTY VAN WITSEN

The Bean Boy

In the years between this and that, there lived a little boy named String, because he used strings for shoelaces: a red string in one shoe and a green string in the other. Now, String lived in a Lima Bean Field. And when the Lima beans were green he picked them, put them in sacks, and took sackfuls of green Lima beans into town to sell, so he was called the Bean Boy.

One morning, when the town looked yellow and dusty as a Chinaman sitting in the sun, String stopped at the Governor's Palace to leave a sack of green Lima beans for the Governor's little daughter, who had ordered large, flat beans in her soup. She was called Dulce because, although her eyes were dark and sad, her smile was sweet and gaudy as a dulce.

Now, Dulce was leaning out of the palace window watching for her sack of large, flat beans, when the Bean Boy came whistling into the patio of the palace, tripping over his red and green shoestrings, always coming undone. Dulce ran downstairs, fetching a pan, so the Bean Boy could dump out his sack of big, flat beans. Then the Bean Boy sat down to tie up his green and red shoestrings. By this time, the Governor's little daughter had stopped smiling, so String noticed how sad and dark her eyes looked.

"It must be nice," she said, "to live in a bean field and bring sacks of beans into town."

"It is nice. And I am always finding things on the way in and out."

"What kind of things?" asked Dulce eagerly.

"Oh, tree toads and moonstones and old Spanish pesos and Indian beads and kelp for dress-up helmets."

At that the Governor's little daughter smiled her gaudy smile. "Maybe," she asked, "maybe you can find my dream for me?"

"Maybe I can," said the Bean Boy.

"I dreamed," Dulce said, "that my father was not a governor any more and didn't need to worry about revolutions. I dreamed that he was an organ-grinder man, with a tiny tomboy monkey from Central America."

The Bean Boy nodded. "I know. And you went with him, walking through bean fields, singing, 'Maria Mia.' And people filled your cup with pennies. And you made a bonfire every night, popping stacks of corn."

"Yes, yes, and my father didn't worry any more about revolutions. Just think, he didn't need to worry about revolutions!"

Dulce opened her sad eyes wide open. "But I only dreamed it once. Now, do you think you can find my dream again for me?"

"Of course." And the Bean Boy took a moonstone, an Indian bead, a tree toad, and an old Spanish coin out of his pocket, spreading them on the tile floor in front of Dulce.

"Of course," said the Bean Boy. "I can find anything on my way in and out."

"Then," said Dulce, "I intend to marry you when you grow up tall."

At that the Bean Boy went whistling away, tying up the green and red strings, always coming undone.

Next morning at sunup, String was picking big, flat beans and putting them into sacks, when a Goblin came hurrying up a bean row and tipped his bean-leaf cap, stuck round with oak holly berries, green and red ones.

"Could you possibly spare two good-sized beans this morning?" the Goblin inquired politely. "The finest baby of our King will be christened in sixteen minutes, and I find myself without a christening present."

The polite Goblin bowed as best he could, for he was a thick little person. He had a wide, cheerful mouth and looked hearty in his seaweed suit.

The Bean Boy was red with surprise.

"Two beans, you want two beans!" he kept saying.

"If you can spare them, please," said the polite Goblin.

"Fill your cap," String told him. And he helped the Goblin pick eight or ten fine Lima beans.

"While you are here," the Bean Boy said hurriedly, "I wish you would tell me where to find the dream of the Governor's little girl, Dulce."

The polite Goblin bowed in spite of his girth. "Certainly," he said, "all dreams are kept in the Cave of Yawns down by the sea, two leagues south, two leagues west. And there you are. But remember not to yawn in the cave. For every time anyone yawns, the cave gets bigger and bigger, opening up at the end. And if you go to sleep in there, you will never wake up. Then," asked the Goblin, "who will pick the beans, put them in sacks, and take sackfuls of Lima beans into town?"

He went away, looking surprised at his own question.

At that the Bean Boy hurried off, going two leagues south, two leagues west. And there he was, at the Cave of Yawns down by the sea. There were dark chests along the walls of the cave. Rich, hand-carved chests, out of which the Sandman was selecting dreams. He stood at the farthest end of the cave, throwing a handful of sand into his bag and then a dream. Just like that—a handful of sand and then a dream. "Whoo, whoo," called the Bean Boy, but when the Sandman looked up the Bean Boy yawned.

The cave opened up at the end just as the polite Goblin said it would. The Sandman was leagues farther away now than he had been before.

The Bean Boy began to feel sleepy now. His hands went to sleep, his feet went to sleep, and every step pricked like pins and needles. Then the Bean Boy yawned again, and the cave opened up at the end, just as the polite Goblin said it would. The Sandman and the rich, hand-carved chests were so far away now, they looked like dots on a dotted line. Then the Bean Boy's ears went to sleep. After that his nose went to sleep. But he said to himself, "Even though I feel all over like a pincushion, I must keep my two eyes awake and walk with my feet asleep until I can nudge the Sandman and get Dulce's dream for her."

So the Bean Boy walked with his feet asleep, his hands asleep, his ears asleep, and his nose asleep. But the jolt of tripping over his shoestrings kept his eyes awake until he nudged the Sandman.

"Please," he said, stifling an enormous yawn, "may I have Dulce's dream?"

"What was it like?" asked the Sandman. "And about how long?"

"Hurry," cried the Bean Boy. "I'm going to yawn again."

"Did it have a monkey and an organ-grinder in it and a song called 'Maria Mia'?"

"Yes, yes." The Bean Boy's eyes were closing. But he tripped over his shoestrings and opened them again with a terrible effort.

"It's an old dream," said the Sandman, "almost worn out, so I suppose you may as well have it." He shook the dream out, sticking his fingers through the holes. The Bean Boy's eyes closed again. He shook himself, saying, "My hands are asleep, my feet are asleep, and so are my nose and ears, but though I feel like a pincushion all over, I must keep my eyes open." So he opened his eyes. The Sandman handed him the old, tattered dream, and the Bean Boy ran from the cave with his feet asleep, his hands asleep, his ears asleep, and his nose asleep. He was really asleep all over, except his eyes were awake from the jolt of tripping over his shoestrings, a red string in one shoe and a green string in the other.

Next morning, before dawn, the little boy started for town with his bean sacks and the old dream, which looked as if it were falling to pieces. When he came near the gates of the town, he heard guns. At that, soldiers came out, singing lustily, "Maria Mia." The Bean Boy went into town. The palace was in ruins, and there on some stones sat the Governor and Dulce.

"We have had another revolution," Dulce told the Bean Boy, who noticed how sad and dark her eyes were.

Just then a soldier came running up and spoke low to the Governor.

"Your Excellency must go away at once in disguise!"

Whereupon the Bean Boy handed Dulce the old, worn dream. And so it happened that the Governor disguised himself as an organ-grinder man, owning a tiny tomboy monkey from Central America. He and Dulce and the Bean Boy wandered up and down the world Joyously, making bonfires every night and popping stacks of corn. After they had wandered from one end of

the world to the other, the Bean Boy married Dulce one night by a big campfire, and they inherited great stretches of bean fields, where they lived happily for years and years and years and years.

MONICA SHANNON

The Baker's New Coat

There was once a village called Chitter Chat because the people who lived there talked so much. They talked and they talked from the time they got up in the morning until they went to bed at night. They talked to each other, and to their cats and their dogs, and their horses and their goats. And if they couldn't find anybody else to talk to they talked to themselves! Mercy, how those people did talk!

But there were two people in the village of Chitter Chat who hardly spoke at all. The first was the Sage. As you know, a sage is a very wise person. This one was most especially wise. He lived off by himself in a little house in the woods. He was an old, old man, with no hair on the top of his head at all. But to make up for that, he had a long gray beard. In fact, it was so long that in winter he used to wrap it three times around his neck and stick the ends in his vest to keep his ears warm. And at night it was most useful too, for then he parted it down the middle and tucked it in on each side to keep out the drafts. In summer he just rolled it up and pinned it tidily with a clothespin so that he wouldn't trip over it. It was only during thunderstorms that the Sage had any real difficulty with his beard, for when the lightning flashed each separate hair stood out full length because of the electricity, so that the poor Sage looked very much like a large hedgehog! Furthermore, if touched at this time, the beard gave off sparks a yard and a quarter long!

In addition to his beard, the Sage had one other treasure, namely, a set of Wise Books. In these books a body could find the answer to any question under the sun. Take a perfectly simple question like, "Why does a duck swim?" All you would have to do would be to look under "Ducks" and there would be the answer, "Because he wants to," plain as plain. Or take a harder one like, "Where does your lap go when you stand up?" Now that is really a hard question. You sit down, and there is your lap in front of you. You stand up, and it's gone! Where did it go to? I'm sure I don't know, but the Wise Books could tell you. Indeed they could!

Naturally the people of Chitter Chat were very proud of their Sage and of his Wise Books. Whenever they needed advice they always went to him and asked him what to do. He always told them, too. However, he had one rule, and that was that he would speak only once in twenty-four hours. He had had to make this rule, you see, for if he hadn't people would have bothered him all the time, for they dearly loved to ask questions!

The other person in Chitter Chat who didn't talk a great deal was Stephen, sometimes called "The Simpleton." He was a young man who was very fond of fishing, which is probably the reason why he was so silent, for catching fish and talking do not go together, as everybody who has tried it knows.

And now I will tell you of the truly dreadful thing that happened to the Baker of Chitter Chat one fine summer morning. It was the twenty-fourth of June, and the twenty-fourth of June was a *very* important day for the Baker. It was the birthday of his Great-Great-Aunt-Mathilda.

Great-Great-Aunt-Mathilda lived in a nearby town called Bubbling Spring which, as you may guess from the name, was famous for a beautiful spring which issued forth from the mountainside and bubbled and boiled merrily from one year's end to the next without ever stopping. Mint and watercress grew along the edges of this spring and not only was the water very delicious but it was also supposed to be unusually pure.

This you will readily believe when I tell you that on this beautiful twenty-fourth of June, Great-Great-Aunt-Mathilda was a hundred and one years old! Think of it, a hundred and *one!* Both the Baker and his wife thought the twenty-fourth of June was the finest day in the year, for it meant that they would put on their best clothes and drive to Bubbling Spring to see Great-Great-Aunt-Mathilda. All her other relatives and friends would be there, and there would be games and ice cream and paper caps for everyone. Of course there was to be a cake. And *what* a cake!

The Baker had been at work on that cake since long before dawn. Each year he made a cake for Great-Great-Aunt-Mathilda's birthday party. It was his present to her, and a fine present it was! It was made of the very best butter and the thickest cream and the sweetest sugar and the freshest eggs, and it was flavored with cinnamon and allspice. Furthermore, it had a cream almond filling, and glistening white frosting on which little pink sugar roses grew. So real were they that a body was tempted to lean over and smell them! . . . Across the beautiful smooth white surface was written in lovely, curlicue letters the words, "A Happy Hundred-and-First Birthday to Great-Great-Aunt-Mathilda."

It was a very large cake, but then Great-Great-Aunt-Mathilda was a very old lady with many, many relatives and friends. When it was finished, the Baker stood back and surveyed it with pride.

"I really think it is my masterpiece," he said to his wife, who had come in to inspect it, "for not only is it perfect in every detail down to the tiniest pink rosebud, but it is as light and airy as sea foam."

"Just as well," said his wife, "otherwise Great-Great-Aunt-Mathilda would not be able to eat any of it. She has only two teeth in her head, the dear woman, and *they* don't meet!"

"She needn't worry. She won't have to chew, for this cake will literally melt in her mouth," said the Baker, as he took off his apron and his high chef's hat and hung them neatly up. "And now I must go and dress for the party. Do you tie up the cake, my dear, and I will carry it out to the cart directly."

So the Baker went upstairs, where his wife had laid out all his clothes for him. As he had taken his bath earlier, he had only to slip them on. First came his fine, ruffled shirt with the lace cuffs. Next his fawn-colored breeches. Those were a little tight in the seat, and the Baker knew that he must be careful not to lean over too suddenly, for fear of accidents.

After the breeches he put on his best cherry-colored waistcoat, and then, last of all, he took up his new coat that he had had made especially for Great-Great-Aunt-Mathilda's party. It was of sky-blue broadcloth with a canary yellow velvet collar and a canary yellow satin lining, and it had crystal buttons that sparkled and glittered like diamonds. Truly it was a coat of coats! The Baker put it on and then stood in front of the mirror and turned this way and that so as to see himself from all angles. Never did a coat fit better and never did a man look happier or handsomer than did the Baker of Chitter Chat with his shining pink cheeks and his jolly blue eyes!

"Hurry, my dear," called his wife.

"I'm coming at once," he answered and, cocking his tall gray hat a little on one side of his head, he first made a perky bow to himself in the mirror, then tucked his cane under his arm and ran down the stairs.

His wife had put the precious cake into a large box tied up in tissue paper and blue ribbon, and had left it on the hall table. The Baker picked it up gingerly, holding the door open with his toe as he did so. Then he edged out, being ever so careful not to jar the box against the doorjamb. But, alas, in spite of his caution, a truly *dreadful* thing happened! The door slammed shut behind him, and as it slammed, it caught the tails of the beautiful, sky-blue coat, caught them and held them tight and fast! There stood the poor Baker on his own threshold, trapped as securely as ever a mouse was trapped!

"Oh dear, oh dear, oh dear!" he cried.

"Whatever is the matter?" called his wife, who was waiting in the cart and had not seen what had happened.

"I'm caught," answered the Baker. "Come quickly, my pet, and open this pesky door!"

So the Baker's wife climbed down out of the cart and hurried up the steps.

"Where is the key?" she asked, for the lock was the kind that locked itself as soon as the door was closed.

"Haven't you got it in your reticule?" asked the Baker.

His wife opened the little black silk bag that she always carried with her and searched thoroughly.

"No," said she, "I have the key to the back door. We must have left the key to the front door inside!"

"Oh, dear, oh, dear, oh, dear, whatever shall I do now?" sighed the Baker.

"First let me take the cake and put it down, out of harm's way, and then we will think of a solution," said his wife, who was a very practical woman. So she took the cake and set it carefully on the top step.

"That's better," said the Baker. He took out his silk handkerchief and wiped his forehead. At this moment the Butcher came by.

"Has something happened?" he said, when he saw the worried looks on the faces of the Baker and his wife. So they explained all about Great-Great-Aunt-Mathilda's party and the cake and the sky-blue coat, and showed him how the tails were caught in the doorjamb, tight as tight.

"Why don't you just slip your arms out and leave the coat hanging there?" suggested the Butcher.

"What! Leave my precious coat, my beautiful sky-blue coat with the canary yellow lining and the crystal buttons? Leave it hanging in the door? Never in the world!" cried the Baker. "Why, why, you can't tell what might happen to it. It might be stolen, or, or someone might drop gooseberry jam on it. At least while I am in it I know it is safe. Besides, I could not possibly go to Great-Great-Aunt-Mathilda's party in my shirt sleeves! It wouldn't be dignified. Suppose I should be called upon to make a speech. Wouldn't *that* be a pretty howdyedo! Whoever heard of a speech in shirt sleeves? No, we will have to think of some better way out than that!"

So they thought.

Presently the Widow and her eleven children came along. Of course they stopped when they saw how unhappy the Butcher and the Baker and his wife looked.

"Whatever is the matter?" they asked, and the Baker's wife told them. The poor Baker was so upset by this time that he could not speak.

"I have a pair of scissors with me. I could snip the tails off and you could sew them on again afterwards, when you had the door opened," said the Widow.

The Baker clutched the tails of his precious coat in alarm. "I will *never* consent to that," he said firmly. *"Never!"*

"I might run to the locksmith and tell him to come and see what he can do," said one of the Widow's children, a boy, the third from the top.

"A fine idea," agreed everyone, and the lad set off for the locksmith as fast as his legs could carry him.

"A clever boy, that," said the Baker to the Widow. "You must be proud of him!"

"He'll pass in a crowd," answered the Widow modestly, but secretly she thought he was quite the brightest boy ever born. In a few minutes he was back . . . without the locksmith.

"Where is the locksmith?" asked the Baker's wife.

"He has the mumps!" said the boy, "and you should see him with his face tied up in flannel soaked in camphorated oil! He looks for all the world like a rabbit with his jaws stuffed full of something!"

"When will he be better?" asked the Widow.

"He can't go out for eight days," the boy replied.

"Eight days! Oh, dear," said the Baker, "I don't see how I can stay here for eight days!"

"I'll bring you out a soft cushion, and it won't be so bad," said his wife.

"But we shall miss Great-Great-Aunt-Mathilda's party!" the Baker sighed, and tears began to roll down his face.

"She'll have another birthday next year, and you'll surely be loose by that time," his wife comforted him.

"You cannot be certain of that," said the Baker, "I mean you cannot be certain that she will have another party. After all, she *is* a hundred and one! No, my dear, there is but one thing to do: you must go alone to the party and carry the cake so that Great-Great-Aunt-Mathilda won't be disappointed. She is counting on that cake, you know!"

"And leave you here all by yourself, stuck in the door? Oh, I couldn't!" exclaimed the Baker's wife.

"But you must!" said the Baker, firmly.

Suddenly another of the Widow's children spoke up, a girl, fourth from the bottom. "Has anyone asked the Sage to look in his Wise Books?" she suggested.

"Why, of course! Why didn't we think of that before?" they all cried. "Do you run, Johnny, and get back as fast as you can so that the Baker and his wife will not be late."

The boy ran off, and everyone cheered up at once. The Sage would certainly be able to tell them exactly the best thing to do.

"Handy things to have around the house, Wise Books," said the Baker.

"Yes, indeed, and isn't it fortunate," suggested his wife, "that the Sage will let us come to him as often as we like, provided we don't come more than once in twenty-four hours?"

They all agreed that this was very fortunate.

Presently Johnny came running back. In his hand he carried a folded paper. "I had him write it down to make certain I'd get it right," he puffed.

"Very intelligent, I'm sure," said the Baker, and the Widow beamed at the praise.

"Read it, then, and be quick about it," cried the Butcher. So the boy opened the paper and began to read.

"Doors, things caught in the jamb of," he read. "When anything gets caught in a doorjamb, great care must be taken in removing it in order to avoid injuring the hinges or marring the paint!" That was what it said. Just that, nothing else!

"I'm afraid that won't be very helpful," sighed the Baker's wife, after a moment during which everybody thought over the Sage's advice. "Not *very* helpful, I'm afraid, for it isn't a question of removing the Baker *carefully*, now, is it? It's a question of removing him at all!"

Once more the tears gathered in the Baker's eyes.

At that very moment who should come strolling by but Stephen, the Simpleton, on his way fishing.

"Hello. What's up?" said he when he saw the Butcher and the Baker and the Baker's wife, and the Widow and the eleven children looking as though it were all the blue Mondays in the year rolled into one. He listened carefully while they explained what had happened.

"You are sure you haven't the key?" he asked.

The Baker's wife looked once more in her reticule, "I have only the key to the back door," she said. "The key to the front door must be on the mantlepiece in the dining room where we always keep it."

"Give me the key to the back door, then," said Stephen.

What ever good will the back door key do when it's the front door the Baker's stuck in? thought the Baker's wife. But she was too polite to say anything. She just handed the Simpleton the key.

He took it and went quickly around the house, whistling merrily. A moment later they heard him in the back hall. Then there was a short silence and then—then they heard the joyful sound of a key turning in the lock of the *front* door!

The next instant the door opened. The Baker was free at last!

"Well, to think it was as easy as all that!" said the Baker and his wife and the Butcher and the Widow and the eleven children. "It just goes to show that if one puts one's mind on a thing and keeps one's temper, even the most difficult problems can be solved!"

Then the Baker and his wife thanked Stephen, the Simpleton, for helping them, and *then* they took the beautiful cake and got into the pretty blue cart and drove to Great-Great-Aunt-Mathilda's hundred and first birthday party, where they had a wonderful time playing games and eating ice cream and cake and wearing paper caps.

Oh, and the cake was every bit as good as it looked, for at the end of the party there wasn't a crumb left, not even enough to feed a wren!

MARGARET CABELL SELF

The White Horse Girl
and the Blue Wind Boy

When the dishes are washed at night time and the cool of the evening has come in summer or the lamps and fires are lit for the night in winter, then the fathers and mothers in the Rootabaga Country sometimes tell the young people the story of the White Horse Girl and the Blue Wind Boy.

The White Horse Girl grew up far in the west of the Rootabaga Country. All the years she grew up as a girl she liked to ride horses. Best of all things for her was to be straddle of a white horse loping with a loose bridle among the hills and along the rivers of the west Rootabaga Country.

She rode one horse white as snow, another horse white as new washed sheep wool, and another white as silver. And she could not tell because she did not know which of these three white horses she liked best.

"Snow is beautiful enough for me any time," she said. "New washed sheep wool, or silver out of a ribbon of the new moon, any or either is white enough for me. I like the white manes, the white flanks, the white noses, the white feet of all my ponies. I like the forelocks hanging down between the white ears of all three—my ponies."

And living neighbor to the White Horse Girl in the same prairie country, with the same black crows flying over their places, was the Blue Wind Boy. All the years he grew up as a boy he liked to walk with his feet in the dirt and the grass, listening to the winds. Best of all things for him was to put on strong shoes

60

and go hiking among the hills and along the rivers of the west Rootabaga Country, listening to the winds.

There was a blue wind of day time, starting sometimes at six o'clock on a summer morning or eight o'clock on a winter morning. And there was a night wind with blue of summer stars in summer and blue of winter stars in winter. And there was yet another, a blue wind of the times between night and day, a blue dawn and evening wind. All three of these winds he liked so well he could not say which he liked best.

"The early morning wind is strong as the prairie and whatever I tell it I know it believes and remembers," he said, "and the night wind with the big dark curves of the night sky in it, the night wind gets inside of me and understands all my secrets. And the blue wind of the times between, in the dusk when it is neither night nor day, this is the wind that asks me questions and tells me to wait and it will bring me whatever I want."

Of course, it happened as it had to happen, the White Horse Girl and the Blue Wind Boy met. She, straddling one of her white horses, and he, wearing his strong hiking shoes in the dirt and the grass, it had to happen they should meet among the hills and along the rivers of the west Rootabaga Country where they lived neighbors.

And of course, she told him all about the snow white horse and the horse white as new washed sheep wool and the horse white as a silver ribbon of the new moon. And he told her all about the blue winds he liked listening to, the early morning wind, the night sky wind, and the wind of the dusk between, the wind that asked him questions and told him to wait.

One day the two of them were gone. On the same day of the week the White Horse Girl and the Blue Wind Boy went away. And their fathers and mothers and sisters and brothers and uncles and aunts wondered about them and talked about them, because they didn't tell anybody beforehand they were going. Nobody at all knew beforehand or afterward why they were going away, the real honest why of it.

They left a short letter. It read:

To All Our Sweethearts, Old Folks and Young Folks:
We have started to go where the white horses come
from and where the blue winds begin. Keep a corner
in your hearts for us while we are gone.

THE WHITE HORSE GIRL

THE BLUE WIND BOY

That was all they had to guess by in the west Rootabaga Country, to guess and guess where two darlings had gone.

Many years passed. One day there came riding across the Rootabaga Country a Gray Man on Horseback. He looked like he had come a long ways. So they asked him the question they always asked of any rider who looked like he had come a long ways, "Did you ever see the White Horse Girl and the Blue Wind Boy?"

"Yes," he answered, "I saw them.

"It was a long, long ways from here I saw them," he went on, "it would take years and years to ride where they are. They were sitting together and talking to each other, sometimes singing, in a place where the land runs high and tough rocks reach up. And they were looking out across water, blue water as far as the eye could see. And away far off the blue waters met the blue sky.

" 'Look!' said the Boy, 'that's where the blue winds begin.'

"And far out on the blue waters, just a little this side of where the blue winds begin, there were white manes, white flanks, white noses, white galloping feet.

" 'Look!' said the Girl, 'that's where the white horses come from.'

"And then nearer to the land came thousands in an hour, millions in a day, white horses, some white as snow, some like new washed sheep wool, some white as silver ribbons of the new moon.

"I asked them, 'Whose place is this?' They answered, 'It belongs to us; this is what we started for; this is where the white horses come from; this is where the blue winds begin.' "

And that was all the Gray Man on Horseback would tell the people of the west Rootabaga Country. That was all he knew, he said, and if there was any more he would tell it.

And the fathers and mothers and sisters and brothers and uncles and aunts of the White Horse Girl and the Blue Wind Boy wondered and talked often about whether the Gray Man on Horseback made up the story out of his head or whether it happened just as he told it.

Anyhow this is the story they tell sometimes to the young people of the west Rootabaga Country when the dishes are washed at night and the cool of the evening has come in summer or the lamps and fires are lit for the night in winter.

CARL SANDBURG

~ Part Two
TO TICKLE
THE FUNNY BONE

The King's Rijstepap*

Once upon a time, long, long ago, the King of the Netherlands sent word to the little village of Onstwedde that he would pay it a visit within a few days.

As the king was well beloved by all his subjects, the farmers of Onstwedde naturally were very much pleased by the coming visit. But how could they show the king that they appreciated this honor? they wondered. They would have liked to present him with a gift, but in the first place they were not very rich, and besides, the king already had everything in the world he wanted.

* Pronounce rice-te-pap (rice-pudding)

The burgomaster called his burghers together, but no one could suggest anything suitable. At last, just as the burgomaster had given up all hope of finding something, he had an idea.

"I know what we can do!" he cried. "You all know how famous our village is for its *rijstepap*. Well, since we are unable to give the king anything of value, let each of us offer him a bowl of our finest *rijstepap*."

The farmers cheerfully agreed, and the next day the town crier announced in the market square that every farmer's wife must prepare a bowl of the best *rijstepap* she could make, for presentation to the king.

The good wives wasted no time in gathering together the necessary ingredients for this favorite Dutch dish—rice, milk and sugar—and on the morning of the king's arrival, all the farmers met at the town hall, each with a bowl of *rijstepap* in his hands.

Now, they were simple folk and had never been in the presence of royalty before, so they asked the burgomaster how to act before his Majesty.

"Oh, I'll go in first, and you follow behind and do exactly as I do," the burgomaster said importantly.

The farmers fell in line and, one by one, followed the burgomaster to the inn where the king was staying.

Everything went well until they reached the inn. But when the burgomaster entered the room where the king was waiting, *zip!* he went over the newly waxed floor, and tumbled plump upon his stomach. Up flew the bowl of *rijstepap* from his hands, landing in a hundred pieces at the king's feet, spattering the royal garments from top to toe.

The farmers thought it was indeed a strange way to welcome royalty, but remembering the burgomaster's instructions to do as he did, they all fell *kerplunk!* on *their* stomachs and *threw* their bowls of *rijstepap* at the king's feet.

The burgomaster grew red with anger and bellowed at the top of his voice to the farmer next to him: "What a *domkop* you are!" The farmers turned to the king and called out good-naturedly: "What a *domkop* you are!" That was too much for the poor burgomaster, and he pounced on his neighbor and soundly boxed his ears. The farmer immediately turned around and boxed the next man's ears. Thus it went on all around the room. Some of the farmers did not take the whacking in the right spirit and before long there was a rough-and-tumble going on under the king's very eyes.

At first the king was very much surprised and more than a little indignant, but after a moment the sight of all these farmers, rice-pudding on their clothes, rice-pudding on their hands and faces, and rice-pudding even in their hair, seemed to him so funny that he began to laugh and laugh, until the tears rolled from his eyes.

Finally the burgomaster caught the farmer nearest to him by the collar and hauled him out of the room, quickly followed by the others. He was thoroughly ashamed of what the king might think of him and his ignorant farmers.

But the king, calling his courtiers together, left the village, still chuckling to himself, and when he arrived at his castle, sent a purse of gold to the burgomaster, to be divided among the farmers in appreciation of the good time he had had at Onst-wedde.

JOHAN HART

Farmer Griggs's Boggart

Did you ever hear of a boggart? No! Then I will tell you. A boggart is a small imp that lives in a man's house, unseen by anyone, doing a little good and much harm. This imp was called a boggart in the old times; now we call such by other names—ill-temper, meanness, uncharitableness, and the like. Even now, they say, you may find a boggart in some houses. There is no placing reliance on a boggart; sometimes he may seem to be of service to his master, but there is no telling when he may do him an ill turn.

Rap! tap! tap! came a knock at the door.

The wind was piping Jack Frost's, for the time was winter, and it blew from the north. The snow lay all over the ground, like soft feathers, and the hayricks looked as though each one wore a dunce cap, like the dull boy in Dame Week's school over by the green. The icicles hung down by the thatch, and the little birds crouched shivering in the bare and leafless hedgerows.

But inside the farmhouse all was warm and pleasant; the great logs snapped and crackled and roared in the wide chimney-place, throwing red light up and down the walls, so that the dark night only looked in through the latticed windows. Farmer Griggs sat warming his knees at the blaze, smoking his pipe in great comfort, while his crock of ale, with three roasted crab apples bobbing about within it, warmed in the hot ashes beside the blazing logs, simmering pleasantly in the ruddy heat.

Dame Griggs's spinning-wheel went humm-m-m! hum-m-m-m-m! like a whole hiveful of bees, the cat purred in the warmth, the dog basked in the blaze, and the little red sparks danced about the dishes standing all along in a row on the dresser.

But, *rap! tap! tap!* came a knock at the door.

Then Farmer Griggs took his pipe from out his mouth. "Did 'ee hear un, dame?" said he. "Zooks now, there be somebody outside the door."

"Well then, thou gert oaf, why don't 'ee let un in?" said Dame Griggs.

"Look 'ee now," said Georgie Griggs to himself, "sure women be of quicker wits than men!" So he opened the door. *Whoo!* In rushed the wind, and the blaze of the logs made as though it would leap up the chimney for fear.

"Will you let me in out of the cold, Georgie Griggs?" piped a small voice. Farmer Griggs looked down and saw a little wight no taller than his knee standing in the snow on the doorstep. His face was as brown as a berry, and he looked up at the farmer with great eyes as bright as those of a toad. The red light of the fine shone on him, and Georgie Griggs saw that his feet were bare and that he wore no coat.

"Who be 'ee, little man?" said Farmer Griggs.

"I'm a boggart, at your service."

"Na, na," said Farmer Griggs, "thee's at na sarvice o' mine. I'll give na room in my house to the likes o' thee"; and he made as though he would have shut the door in the face of the little urchin.

"But listen, Georgie Griggs," said the boggart; "I will do you a good service."

Then Farmer Griggs did listen. "What sarvice will 'ee do me, then?" said he.

"I'll tend your fires," said the manikin, "I'll bake your bread, I'll wash your dishes, I'll scour your pans, I'll scrub your floors, I'll brew your beer, I'll roast your meat, I'll boil your water, I'll stuff your sausages, I'll skim your milk, I'll make your butter, I'll press your cheese, I'll pluck your geese, I'll spin your thread, I'll knit your stockings, I'll mend your clothes, I'll patch your shoes—I'll be everywhere and do all of the work in your house, so that you will not have to give so much as a groat for wages to cook, scullion, or serving wench!"

Then Farmer Griggs listened a little longer without shutting the door, and so did Dame Griggs. "What's thy name, boggart?" said he.

"Hardfist," said the boggart; and he came a little farther in at the door, for he saw that Farmer Griggs had a mind to let him in all of the way.

"I don't know," said Georgie Griggs, scratching his head doubtfully; "it's an ill thing, lettin' mischief intull the house! Thee's better outside, I doubt."

"Shut the door, Georgie!" called out Dame Griggs; "thou'rt lettin' th' cold air intull th' room."

Then Farmer Griggs shut the door, but the boggart was on the inside.

This is the way in which the boggart came into Farmer Griggs's house, and there he was to stay, for it is no such easy matter getting rid of the likes of him when we once let him in, I can tell you.

The boggart came straightway over to the warm fire, and the dog growled—*"chur-r-r-r!"*—and showed his teeth, and the cat spit anger and jumped up on the dresser, with her back arched and her tail on end. But the boggart cared never a whit for this, but laid himself comfortably down among the warm ashes.

Now imps, like this boggart, can only be seen as the frost is seen—when it is cold. So as he grew warmer and warmer, he grew thin, like a jellyfish, and at last, when he had become thoroughly warmed through, Farmer Griggs and the dame could see him no more than though he was thin air. But he was in the house, and he stayed there, I can tell you. For a time everything went as smooth as cream; all of the work of the house was done as though by magic, for the boggart did all that he had promised; he made the fires, he baked the bread, he washed the dishes, he scoured the pans, he scrubbed the floors, he brewed the beer, he roasted the meat, he stuffed the sausages, he skimmed the milk, he made the butter, he pressed the cheese, he plucked the geese, he spun the thread, he knit the stockings, he mended the clothes, he patched the shoes—he was everywhere and did all of the work of the house. When Farmer Griggs saw these things done, and so deftly, he rubbed his hands and chuckled to himself. He sent

cook and scullion and serving maid a-packing, there being nothing for them to do, for, as I said, all of these things were done as
smooth as cream. But after a time, and when the boggart's place
had become easy to him, like an old shoe, mischief began to play
the pipes and he began to show his pranks. The first thing that he
did was to scrape the farmer's butter, so that it was light of
weight, and all of the people of the market town hooted at him for
giving less than he sold. Then he skimmed the children's milk, so
that they had nothing but poor watery stuff to pour over their
pottage of a morning. He took the milk from the cat, so that it

was like to starve; he even pilfered the bones and scrapings of the
dishes from the poor house-dog, as though he was a very magpie.
He blew out the rushlights, so that they were all in the dark after
sunset; he made the fires burn cold, and played a hundred and
forty other impish tricks of the like kind. As for the poor little
children, they were always crying and complaining that the
boggart did this and the boggart did that; that he scraped the
butter from their bread and pulled the coverlids off of them at
night.

Still the boggart did his work well, and so Farmer Griggs put
up with his evil ways as long as he could. At last the time came
when he could bear it no longer. "Look 'ee, now, Mally," said he

to his dame, "it's all along o' thee that this trouble's coome intull th' house. I'd never let the boggart in with my own good-will!" So spoke Farmer Griggs, for even nowadays there are men here and there who will now and then lay their own bundle of faults on their wives' shoulders.

"I bade thee do naught but shut the door!" answered Dame Griggs.

"Ay; it's easy enough to shut the door after the trouble's come in!"

"Then turn it out again!"

"Turn un out! Odds bodkins, that's woman's wit! Dost 'ee not see that there's no turnin' o' un out? Na, na; there's naught to do but to go out ourselves!"

Yes; there was nothing else to be done. Go they must, if they would be rid of the boggart. So one fine bright day in the blessed springtime, they packed all of their belongings into a great wain, or cart, and set off to find a new home.

Off they trudged, the three little children seated high up in the wain, and the farmer and the dame plodding ahead.

Now, as they came to the bottom of Shooter's Hill, whom should they meet but their good neighbor and gossip, Jerry Jinks. "So, Georgie," said he, "you're leavin' th' ould house at last?"

"High, Jerry," quoth Georgie. "We were forced tull it, neighbor, for that black boggart torments us so that there was no rest night or day for it. The poor bairns' stomachs are empty, and the good dame's nigh dead for it. So off we go, like th' fieldfares in the autumn—we're flittin', we're flittin'!"

Now on the wain was a tall, upright churn. As soon as Georgie had ended his speech, the lid of the churn began to clipper-clapper, and who should speak out of it but the boggart himself. "Ay, Jerry, we're a flittin', we're a flittin', man! Good-day to ye, neighbor, good-day to ye! Come and see us soon time!"

"High!" cried Georgie Griggs, "art thou there, thou black imp? Dang un! We'll all go back tull th' old house, for sure it's better to bear trouble there than in a new place."

So back they went again—boggart and all.

By this you may see, my dear, if you warm an imp by your fire, he will soon turn the whole house topsy-turvy. Likewise, one cannot get rid of a boggart by going from here to there, for it is sure to be in the cart with the household things.

But how did Georgie Griggs get rid of his boggart? That I will tell you.

He went to Father Grimes, the wise man, who lived on in a little house on the moor. "Father Grimes," said he, "how shall I get rid of my boggart?"

Then Father Grimes told him to take this and that, and to do thus and so with them, and see what followed. So Farmer Griggs went to Hugh the tailor's, and told him to make a pretty red coat and a neat pair of blue breeches. Then he went to William the hatter's, and bade him to make a nice little velvet cap with a bell at the top of it. Then he went to Thomas the shoemaker's, and bade him to make a fine little pair of shoes. So they all did as he told them, and after these things were made he took them home with him. He laid them on a warm spot on the hearth where the boggart used to come to sleep at night. Then he and his dame hid in the closet to see what would follow.

Presently came the boggart, whisking here and dancing there, though neither the farmer nor the dame could see him any more than though he had been a puff of wind.

"Heigh-ho!" cried the boggart, "these be fine things for sure." So saying, he tried the hat upon his head, and it fitted exactly. Then he tried the coat on his shoulders, and it fitted like wax. Then he tried the breeches on his legs, and they fitted as though they grew there. Then he tried the shoes on his feet, and there never was such a fit. So he was clad in all his new clothes from top to toe, whereupon he began dancing until he made the ashes on the hearth spin around with him as though they had gone mad, and, as he danced, he sang:

Cap for the head, alas poor head!
Coat for the back, alas poor back!
Breeks for the legs, alas poor legs!

Shoen for the feet, alas poor feet!
If these be mine, mine cannot be
The house of honest man, Georgie!

So he went singing and dancing, and skipping and leaping, out of the house and away. As for Georgie Griggs and his dame, they never heard a squeak from him afterwards.

Thus it was that Farmer Griggs got rid of his boggart. All I can say is, that if I could get rid of mine as easily (for I have one in my own house), I would make him a suit of clothes of the finest silks and satins, and would hang a bell of pure silver on the point of his cap. But, alackaday! there are no more wise men left to us, like good Father Grimes, to tell one an easy way to get rid of one's boggart.

HOWARD PYLE

The Three Sillies

Once upon a time there was a farmer and his wife who had one daughter, and she was courted by a gentleman. Every evening he used to come and see her, and stop to supper at the farmhouse, and the daughter used to be sent down into the cellar to draw the beer for supper. So one evening she had gone down to draw the beer, and she happened to look up at the ceiling while she was drawing, and she saw a mallet stuck in one of the beams. It must have been there a long, long time, but somehow or other she had never noticed it before, and she began a-thinking. And she thought it was very dangerous to have that mallet there, for she said to herself: "Suppose him and me was to be married, and we was to have a son, and he was to grow up to be a man, and come down into the cellar to draw the beer, like as I'm doing now, and the mallet was to fall on his head and kill him, what a dreadful thing it would be!" And she put down the candle and the jug, and sat herself down and began a-crying.

Well, they began to wonder upstairs how it was that she was so long drawing the beer, and her mother went down to see after her, and she found her sitting on the settle crying, and the beer running over the floor. "Why, whatever is the matter?" said her mother.

"Oh, mother!" says she, "look at that horrid mallet! Suppose we was to be married, and was to have a son, and he was to grow up, and was to come down to the cellar to draw the beer, and the mallet was to fall on his head and kill him, what a dreadful thing it would be!"

"Dear, dear! what a dreadful thing it would be!" said the

mother, and she sat her down aside of the daughter and started a-crying too.

Then after a bit the father began to wonder that they didn't come back, and he went down into the cellar to look after them himself, and there they two sat a-crying, and the beer running all over the floor. "Whatever is the matter?" says he.

"Why," says the mother, "look at that horrid mallet. Just suppose, if our daughter and her sweetheart was to be married, and was to have a son, and he was to grow up, and was to come down into the cellar to draw the beer, and the mallet was to fall on his head and kill him, what a dreadful thing it would be!"

"Dear, dear, dear! so it would!" said the father, and he sat himself down aside of the other two, and started a-crying.

Now the gentleman got tired of stopping up in the kitchen by himself, and at last he went down into the cellar too, to see what they were after; and there they three sat a-crying side by side, and the beer running all over the floor. And he ran straight and turned the tap. Then he said: "Whatever are you three doing, sitting there crying, and letting the beer run all over the floor?"

"Oh!" says the father, "look at that horrid mallet! Suppose you and our daughter was to be married, and was to have a son, and he was to grow up, and was to come down into the cellar to draw the beer, and the mallet was to fall on his head and kill him!" And then they all started a-crying worse than before.

But the gentleman burst out a-laughing, and reached up and pulled out the mallet, and then he said, "I've traveled many miles, and I never met three such big sillies as you three before; and now I shall start out on my travels again, and when I can find three bigger sillies than you three, then I'll come back and marry your daughter." So he wished them good-bye, and started off on his travels, and left them all crying because the girl had lost her sweetheart.

Well, he set out, and he traveled a long way, and at last he came to a woman's cottage that had some grass growing on the roof. And the woman was trying to get her cow to go up a ladder to the grass, and the poor thing durst not go. So the gentleman asked the woman what she was doing.

"Why, lookye," she said, "look at all that beautiful grass. I'm going to get the cow on to the roof to eat it. She'll be quite safe, for I shall tie a string round her neck, and pass it down the chimney, and tie it to my wrist as I go about the house, so she can't fall off without my knowing it."

"Oh, you poor silly!" said the gentleman, "you should cut the grass and throw it down to the cow!" But the woman thought it was easier to get the cow up the ladder than to get the grass down, so she pushed her and coaxed her and got her up, and tied a string round her neck, and passed it down the chimney, and fastened it to her own wrist. And the gentleman went on his way, but he hadn't gone far when the cow tumbled off the roof, and hung by the string tied round her neck, and it strangled her. And the weight of the cow tied to her wrist pulled the woman up the chimney, and she stuck fast halfway and was smothered in the soot.

Well, that was one big silly.

And the gentleman went on and on, and he went to an inn to stop the night, and they were so full at the inn that they had to put him in a double-bedded room, and another traveler was to sleep in the other bed. The other man was a very pleasant fellow, and they got very friendly together; but in the morning, when they were both getting up, the gentleman was surprised to see the other hang his trousers on the knobs of the chest of drawers and run across the room and try to jump into them, and he tried over and over again, and couldn't manage it; and the gentleman wondered whatever he was doing it for. At last he stopped and wiped his face with his handkerchief. "Oh dear," he says, "I do think trousers are the most awkwardest kind of clothes that ever were. I can't think who could have invented such things. It takes me the best part of an hour to get into mine every morning, and I get so hot! How do you manage yours?" So the gentleman burst out a-laughing, and showed him how to put them on; and he was very much obliged to him, and said he never should have thought of doing it that way.

So that was another big silly.

Then the gentleman went on his travels again; and he came to a village, and outside the village there was a pond, and round the pond was a crowd of people. And they had got rakes, and brooms, and pitchforks, reaching into the pond; and the gentleman asked what was the matter. "Why," they say, "matter enough! Moon's tumbled into the pond, and we can't rake her out anyhow!" So the gentleman burst out a-laughing, and told them to look up in the sky, and that it was only the shadow in the water. But they wouldn't listen to him, and abused him shamefully, and he got away as quick as he could.

So there was a whole lot of sillies bigger than them three sillies at home. So the gentleman turned back home again and married the farmer's daughter, and if they didn't live happy for ever after, that's nothing to do with you or me.

JOSEPH JACOBS

The Cat and the Parrot

Once there was a cat and a parrot. And they had agreed to ask each other to dinner, turn and turn about: first the cat should ask the parrot, then the parrot should invite the cat, and so on. It was the cat's turn first.

Now the cat was very mean. He provided nothing at all for dinner except a pint of milk, a little slice of fish, and a biscuit. The parrot was too polite to complain, but he did not have a very good time.

When it was his turn to invite the cat, he cooked a fine dinner. He had a roast of meat, a pot of tea, a basket of fruit, and, best of

all, he baked a whole clothesbasketful of little cakes!—little, brown, crispy, spicy cakes! Oh, I should say as many as five hundred. And he put four hundred and ninety-eight of the cakes before the cat, keeping only two for himself.

Well, the cat ate the roast, and drank the tea, and sucked the fruit, and then he began on the pile of cakes. He ate all the four hundred and ninety-eight cakes, and then he looked round and said, "I'm hungry; haven't you anything to eat?"

"Why," said the parrot, "here are my two cakes, if you want them?"

The cat ate up the two cakes, and then he licked his chops and said, "I am beginning to get an appetite; have you anything to eat?"

"Well, really," said the parrot, who was now rather angry, "I don't see anything more, unless you wish to eat me!" He thought the cat would be ashamed when he heard that—but the cat just looked at him and licked his chops again—and slip! slop! gobble! down his throat went the parrot!

Then the cat started down the street. An old woman was standing by, and she had seen the whole thing, and she was shocked that the cat should eat his friend. "Why, cat!" she said, "how dreadful of you to eat your friend the parrot!"

"Parrot, indeed!" said the cat. "What's a parrot to me? I've a great mind to eat you, too." And—before you could say "Jack Robinson"—slip! slop! gobble! down went the old woman!

Then the cat started down the road again, walking like this, because he felt so fine. Pretty soon he met a man driving a donkey. The man was beating the donkey, to hurry him up, and when he saw the cat he said, "Get out of my way, cat; I'm in a hurry and my donkey might tread on you."

"Donkey, indeed!" said the cat, "much I care for a donkey! I have eaten five hundred cakes, I've eaten my friend the parrot, I've eaten an old woman—what's to hinder my eating a miserable man and a donkey?"

And slip! slop! gobble! down went the old man and the donkey.

Then the cat walked on down the road, jauntily, like this.

After a little, he met a procession, coming that way. The king was at the head, walking proudly with his newly married bride, and behind him were his soldiers, marching, and behind them were ever and ever so many elephants, walking two by two. The king felt very kind to everybody, because he had just been married, and he said to the cat, "Get out of my way, pussy, get out of my way—my elephants might hurt you."

"Hurt me!" said the cat, shaking his fat sides. "Ho, ho! I've eaten five hundred cakes, I've eaten my friend the parrot, I've eaten an old woman, I've eaten a man and a donkey; what's to hinder my eating a beggarly king?"

And slip! slop! gobble! down went the king; down went the queen; down went the soldiers—and down went all the elephants!

Then the cat went on, more slowly; he had really had enough to eat, now. But a little farther on he met two land crabs, scuttling along in the dust. "Get out of our way, pussy," they squeaked.

"Ho, ho, ho!" cried the cat in a terrible voice. "I've eaten five hundred cakes, I've eaten my friend the parrot, I've eaten an old woman, a man with a donkey, a king, a queen, his men-at-arms, and all his elephants; and now I'll eat you too."

And slip! slop! gobble! down went the two land crabs.

When the land crabs got down inside, they began to look around. It was very dark, but they could see the poor king sitting in a corner with his bride on his arm; she had fainted. Near them were the men-at-arms, treading on one another's toes, and the elephants still trying to form in twos—but they couldn't because there was not room. In the opposite corner sat the old woman, and near her stood the man and his donkey. But in the other corner was a great pile of cakes, and by them perched the parrot, his feathers all drooping.

"Let's get to work!" said the land crabs. And snip, snap, they began to make a little hole in the side, with their sharp claws. Snip, snap, snip, snap—till it was big enough to get through. Then out they scuttled.

Then out walked the king, carrying his bride; out marched the men-at-arms; out tramped the elephants, two by two; out came the old man, beating his donkey; out walked the old woman, scolding the cat; and last of all, out hopped the parrot, holding a cake in each claw. (You remember, two cakes was all he wanted?)

But the poor cat had to spend the whole day sewing up the hole in his coat!

SARA CONE BRYANT

The Most Magnificent Cook of All

Once upon a time this happened—in fact so long ago that no one knows when it did happen. The Town of Kampen was then standing, and was ruled over by a burgomaster helped in his hard task by a town council.

Then and there dwelt a very skillful cook. Better than all the confectioners and cooks of his time did he understand broiling and boiling, roasting and toasting, stewing and brewing, the beating of sauces and the mixing of gravies, the turning of meats on spits, and the roasting of baby pigs. When, with a careless air, he tossed a piece of butter into the hot pan, it spread melting and hissing, and gave forth an odor sweeter than the breath of rose and jasmine.

And not only could he cook the usual things better than others could, but he was able to invent new dishes. He was in fact an artist of a cook! His fancy cakes stood up on the platters like towers, their pinnacles adorned with fine pastry of many colors, with frostings and fruits—delicious enough to make a sick man dance in bed!

And what delicate secrets lay hidden in that cook's confections and dishes! Did he not know the flavors of many flowers? Did he not know the strength of herbs and spices—of mace, of thyme, of pepper, of bay leaf, of cinnamon, of vanilla, of aniseed, of mustard, of lemon peel, and of curry? What a man!

One day word arrived that a mighty knight with his followers was coming to visit Kampen. That knight was full of glee, for he well knew what extra good things to eat would await him there. His eyes glistened thinking about them. Indeed, he thought about them every day and a great deal of the night.

The burgomaster and the councilmen of the Town Council of Kampen called the cook. They wished to consult him about the bill of fare. He came, the fat of his body shaking and quaking, and stood before the green council table.

"Friend," said the burgomaster graciously, "we have sent for you, that you may deliberate with our Worshipful Selves on what we shall give the noble knight to eat. It does not make any difference how many ducats are spent. Anything that grows in the field, feeds in the meadow, flies through the air, creeps through the wood, or swims in river or brook, you may cook, if suitable— but under one condition. It must be delicious."

"Father of this Town!" answered the cook solemnly, drawing the nail of his thumb across the sharp butcher's knife he carried, "What do you say to a fat pullet, roasted three quarters of an hour by the town sundial? It shall be done to a turn, basted with fresh butter, its breast delicately browned. I will serve it with a blooming border of fruit."

"That is good," nodded the burgomaster. "Of what more can you think?"

The cook bowed as low as his round fat body would let him.

"A broiled steak coated with pure olive oil. Over a blazing fire of beechwood will I lay the gridiron. I will wait, noble gentlemen, till the meat is done just enough! Trust me! It shall be done to a turn! that noble meat!"

"And what kind of a vegetable?" asked the burgomaster hesitatingly.

"Green peas, of course!" answered the cook reproachfully, "with parsley turned in hot butter."

"And the fish?" said the burgomaster, smacking his lips.

"The fish? Sturgeon, of course!"

"Sturgeon?"

"Sturgeon! Nothing more or less than sturgeon. We have caught one four ells and a half long. And our net, how it shook when we hauled the monster out of the deep!"

The cook's little eyes seemed to swim in his puffy face, then he bent forward and whispered, "O noble gentlemen! Do you know the roe of this fish, called caviar? Caviar prepared my way! Ah! Beaten with little twigs! Just the right amount of salt! Strained! Liquid, liquid it must be, black liquid!"

After the burgomaster and council heard this, they were silent a long time in respect to such an artist of a cook! At last one of the councilmen felt that he must ask just a little question.

"And the soup, Cook! Have you forgotten the soup?"

"Forgotten! I would as soon die! The proper dishes shall be served in their order on the bill of fare. The knight and his train shall not say that we here in Kampen are stupid. For a soup I suggest a clear one of chicken flavored with fragrant herbs."

"Stop! stop! My stomach groans at the thought of waiting," cried the burgomaster, jumping up to embrace the cook. "Just one thing more. . . . What is your dessert?"

"Charlotte russe and macaroons!" cried the cook in triumph.

Then all the councilmen wept with rapture. For compared with this feast, the dinners of other towns were mere victuals.

Everybody in Kampen waited with impatience for the coming of the guest and his followers.

The cook hurried to make ready. He tied on the whitest of snow-white linen aprons, and around his huge body fastened a leather belt, from which hung the knife to butcher the sturgeon. As for the sturgeon, it had been plunged into a large tub of cold water. There it was swimming cheerfully around and around, not knowing what was going to happen. Every few minutes the cook ran to look at it.

The fire flamed up bright enough. It was time to begin.

Hardly had the cook stretched out his hand to grasp the fish when a messenger came running and racing from the town hall.

"Unlucky one!" he shouted. "Be careful what you do! Come first to the noble councilmen. They . . ."

"What is the matter?" asked the cook, much alarmed.

"Matter enough! Go, hear it for yourself! I am not able to say it!"

The cook ran as fast as his fat would let him, till he reached

the town hall. He hurried into the council chamber. There sat the town council in sackcloth and ashes.

"Gentlemen! gentlemen!" gurgled he. "What is it?"

"Cook," said the burgomaster, "you need do no cooking. Our guest stays at home—with a—with a—stomach-ache."

"Will he come soon?"

"As soon as the stomach-ache is over. It may last a week—a month—a year."

"O honorable gentlemen! What shall I do with the sturgeon?"

"With the sturgeon? As soon as the stomach-ache is over . . ."

"But the sturgeon may die! It can remain alive only in fresh water, and when fed with noble carp. Alas! Ah me! We may have to be satisfied with simple trench or bass, with perch or pike, with eels or roach!" This the cook cried out in bitter mockery. Every one present, pitying his grief, bowed the head.

"And the caviar!" the cook went on weeping. "Is there a single fellow-cook in the world, who knows, as I do, what good caviar is? My caviar is like a dark sea that the sunlight cannot pierce! Ah! the purple reflections in my caviar, which . . . How I rave!"

"Cook," said the burgomaster much moved, "is there no way to keep this sturgeon alive till our guest comes?"

The cook shook his head gloomily. "That is not possible."

Then all the councilmen sat silent. Flashed through their dark thoughts the words *sturgeon, caviar.* Evening came on. The cook sighed. The chairman roused himself from deep thought, pushed back his seat from the table, and spoke.

"Honorable gentlemen," he said softly, "I have found no means."

Then lifted the oldest councilman his wise head, and said, "When danger is great, simple talent will not help. Then necessity calls for a genius. The Town of Kampen possesses as many talented folk as there are inhabitants. There exists in Kampen only one genius—that is I.

"Well then, *I* have found a means. Let the sturgeon swim away in the river where it can feed on the noblest carp and grow in weight. When the mighty knight comes with his train, we have only to cast out our net and catch our sturgeon. How can this be, you ask? Well—*we will tie bells to the sturgeon!*"

The cook jumped for joy. The burgomaster did not know whom to press to his heart first. All the folk of Kampen went wild with delight. Everybody ran along with the cook. They wound a string hung with little bells about the body of the sturgeon. The fish did not object.

"It does not know what is happening to it!" laughed everybody.

After that, in stately procession, they carried the sturgeon to the river, and threw it through the air far out into the stream. *Rinkle-tinkle-tinkle,* rang the little bells as the sturgeon struck the water. Immediately the fish dived under, and no one saw it again.

For a long time after that the cook and the Kampen folk listened to hear the tinkling of the bells. Ha! ha! they were sure when that stomach-ache was over, and the noble knight with his train should come, that they would hear the bells and catch the sturgeon. Then the noble knight might feast on fish and caviar. Ha! ha!

And some bad folk yet say that in Kampen Town, the people are still leaning over the railing of the bridge, listening and listening for the *jingle-jingle-jingle* of the bells tied to the Kampen sturgeon.

FRANCES JENKINS OLCOTT

The Three Wishes

Once upon a time, and be sure 'twas a long time ago, there lived a poor woodman in a great forest, and every day of his life he went out to fell timber. So one day he started out, and the goodwife filled his wallet and slung his bottle on his back, that he might have meat and drink in the forest. He had marked out a huge old oak, which, thought he, would furnish many and many a good plank. And when he was come to it, he took his axe in his hand and swung it round his head as though he were minded to fell the tree at one stroke. But he hadn't given one blow, when what should he hear but the pitifullest entreating, and there stood before him a fairy who prayed and beseeched him to spare the tree. He was dazed, as you may fancy, with wonderment and affright, and he couldn't open his mouth to utter a word. But he found his tongue at last, and, "Well," said he, "I'll e'en do as thou wishest."

"You've done better for yourself than you know," answered the fairy, "and to show I'm not ungrateful, I'll grant you your next three wishes, be they what they may." And therewith the fairy was no more to be seen, and the woodman slung his wallet over his shoulder and his bottle at his side, and off he started home.

But the way was long, and the poor man was regularly dazed with the wonderful thing that had befallen him, and when he got home there was nothing in his noddle but the wish to sit down and rest. Maybe, too, 'twas a trick of the fairy's. Who can tell? Anyhow down he sat by the blazing fire, and as he sat he waxed hungry, though it was a long way off suppertime yet.

"Hasn't thou naught for supper, dame?" said he to his wife.

91

"Nay, not for a couple of hours yet," said she.

"Ah!" groaned the woodman, "I wish I'd a good link of sausage here before me."

No sooner had he said the word, when *clatter, clatter, rustle, rustle,* what should come down the chimney but a link of the finest sausage the heart of man could wish for.

If the woodman stared, the goodwife stared three times as much. "What's all this?" says she.

Then all the morning's work came back to the woodman, and he told his tale right out, from beginning to end, and as he told it the goodwife glowered and glowered, and when he had made an end of it she burst out, "Thou be'st but a fool, Jan, thou be'st but a fool, and I wish the sausage were at thy nose, I do indeed."

And before you could say Jack Robinson, there the goodman sat and his nose was the longer for a noble link of sausage.

He gave a pull, but it stuck, and she gave a pull, but it stuck, and they both pulled till they had nigh pulled the nose off, but it stuck and stuck.

"What's to be done now?" said he.

" 'Tisn't so very unsightly," said she, looking hard at him.

Then the woodman saw that if he wished, he must needs wish in a hurry; and wish he did, that the sausage might come off his nose. Well! there it lay in a dish on the table, and if the goodman and goodwife didn't ride in a golden coach, or dress in silk and satin, why, they had at least as fine a sausage for their supper as the heart of man could desire.

JOSEPH JACOBS

Lazy Jack

Once upon a time there was a boy whose name was Jack, and he lived with his mother on a common. They were very poor, and the old woman got her living by spinning, but Jack was so lazy that he would do nothing but bask in the sun in the hot weather, and sit by the corner of the hearth in the wintertime. So they called him Lazy Jack. His mother could not get him to do anything for her, and at last told him, one Monday, that if he did not begin to work for his porridge she would turn him out to get his living as he could.

This roused Jack, and he went out and hired himself for the next day to a neighboring farmer for a penny; but as he was coming home, never having had any money before, he lost it in passing over a brook. "You stupid boy," said his mother, "you should have put it in your pocket."

"I'll do so another time," replied Jack.

On Wednesday, Jack went out again and hired himself to a cow-keeper, who gave him a jar of milk for his day's work. Jack took the jar and put it into the large pocket of his jacket, spilling it all long before he got home. "Dear me!" said the old woman; "you should have carried it on your head."

"I'll do so another time," said Jack.

So on Thursday, Jack hired himself again to a farmer, who agreed to give him a cream cheese for his services. In the evening Jack took the cheese, and went home with it on his head. By the time he got home the cheese was all spoilt, part of it being lost, and part matted with his hair. "You stupid lout," said his mother, "you should have carried it very carefully in your hands."

"I'll do so another time," replied Jack.

On Friday, Lazy Jack again went out, and hired himself to a baker, who would give him nothing for his work but a large tomcat. Jack took the cat and began carrying it very carefully in his hands, but in a short time pussy scratched him so much that he was compelled to let it go. When he got home, his mother said to him, "You silly fellow, you should have tied it with a string, and dragged it along after you."

"I'll do so another time," said Jack.

So on Saturday, Jack hired himself to a butcher, who rewarded him with the handsome present of a shoulder of mutton. Jack took the mutton, tied it to a string, and trailed it along after him in the dirt, so that by the time he had got home the meat was completely spoilt. His mother was this time quite out of patience with him, for the next day was Sunday, and she was obliged to do with cabbage for her dinner. "You ninney-hammer," said she to her son; "you should have carried it on your shoulder."

"I'll do so another time," replied Jack.

On the next Monday, Lazy Jack went once more, and hired himself to a cattle-keeper, who gave him a donkey for his trouble. Jack found it hard to hoist the donkey on his shoulders, but at last he did it, and began walking slowly home with his prize. Now it happened that in the course of his journey there lived a rich man with his only daughter, a beautiful girl, but deaf and dumb. Now she had never laughed in her life, and the doctors said she would never speak till somebody made her laugh. This young lady happened to be looking out of the window when Jack was passing with the donkey on his shoulders, with the legs sticking up in the air, and the sight was so comical and strange that she burst out into a great fit of laughter, and immediately recovered her speech and hearing. Her father was overjoyed, and fulfilled his promise by marrying her to Lazy Jack, who was thus made a rich gentleman. They lived in a large house, and Jack's mother lived with them in great happiness until she died.

JOSEPH JACOBS

The Magic Dumplings

Once upon a time in the village of Wang-Family-Dog's-Tooth, there lived a poor widow and her only son, together with their dog and cat. The son was good and industrious. But though he worked hard early and late and gave all that he earned to his mother, they had little to eat and often went cold and hungry.

One day while her son was away, there came a knocking at the door of their little hut built of rice-straw. The widow Wang opened it, and there stood an old man with an alms-bowl in his hand.

"May the Five Blessings descend upon this House," said he, "longevity, riches, health, love of virtue, and natural death."

"I am sorry," answered she sadly, thinking that he wished alms, "there is no food in this house. Indeed, we have had nothing to eat today. Just see my cat there, how thin she is, and that dog, how his bones stand out."

"I did not come to ask for food," said the old man, smiling, "but because this is a worthy house. You have been a good mother, and your son is filial and industrious. Therefore I am come to help you."

"Are you laughing at me?" asked the Widow Wang, as she looked curiously at the beggar's rags.

"Indeed I am not!" exclaimed the old man, holding out to her a golden charm. "Take this. Whenever you wish something to eat, put it into a pot full of water. Cover the pot. Stand it over the fire. Then say:

Dumplings, Dumplings, piping hot!
Dumplings, Dumplings, fill the pot!

97

"After that, see what comes to pass. And may you have happiness like the Eastern Sea, and longevity like the Southern Mountain."

With these words the old man dropped the golden charm into her hand and vanished. She knew at once that he was really a good fairy.

The Widow Wang hurried to build a fire. She put the golden charm into a pot, covered it, and set it on to boil. Then she cried out in a trembling voice:

Dumplings, Dumplings, piping hot!
Dumplings, Dumplings, fill the pot!

After a moment, in great excitement, she lifted the cover a little. Oh! what a delicious odor poured forth. Oh! how many plump pork dumplings were bobbing around in the bubbling water. She had never seen so many.

"Meat dumplings! Meat dumplings!" she shouted.

She ate and ate till she could hold no more. She fed the dog, and then the cat. They leaped around her with joy, so perfectly cooked, so rich and mouth-watering were those pork dumplings!

When her son came in tired and hungry, she set the covered pot on the fire, and to his surprise he heard her say:

Dumplings, Dumplings, piping hot!
Dumplings, Dumplings, fill the pot!

The next moment she placed before him a large platter heaped high with steaming hot pork dumplings. He ate and ate till he could not swallow another mouthful. After that she told him about the good fairy and his gift of the golden charm.

"And it is because you are such a kind son," said she, "that the good fairy has given it to us."

For some time the Widow Wang and her son, with their dog and cat, lived in ease and comfort. The widow, who was filled with pride, began to ask in her neighbors and treat them to feasts of pork dumplings.

One day Mr. and Mrs. Chang from the village of Duck's-Nest-of-the-Chang-Family, came to the village of Wang-Family-Dog's-Tooth to visit the Widow Wang. Such a feast of dumplings, hot and steaming, as the Widow Wang set before them! They had never tasted anything so good before. In fact, they praised her cooking so much that the Widow Wang swelled with even greater pride and whispered to them the secret of the golden charm. Filled with envy, Mr. and Mrs. Chang went home determined by hook or crook to get possession of it.

One morning while the Widow Wang and her son were away from home, Mrs. Chang slyly crept into the little house of rice-straw, and finding the golden charm, ran off with it. No one saw her except the dog, who was lying in his corner. When the Widow Wang came back, she began to get supper and looked high and low for the golden charm. It was gone! She burst into loud weeping.

When her son came home, she told him that their treasure was lost. Together they hunted everywhere, but they could not find it. All that night the Widow Wang wept loudly, no matter what her son did to comfort her.

After that there was nothing but hunger and cold in the little house of rice-straw, and, of course, no more feastings and callings in of the neighbors. The dog and cat grew thinner and thinner, and the Widow Wang and her son, sadder and sadder.

One day the dog began to leap about and said to the cat, "I have a wonderful idea! Do you suppose that all those delicious pork dumplings were made by means of the golden charm that Mrs. Chang stole?"

"What do you mean?" asked the cat. "Why did you not tell me before that Mrs. Chang had stolen the golden charm?"

"I did not know it at first," said the dog. "I thought she was borrowing it. Just think, perhaps Mr. and Mrs. Chang are feasting tonight on our pork dumplings!"

"They shall not feast long," said the cat, "if you are willing to help me get back the golden charm."

"Yes, indeed," said the dog. "I will help, but what can I do?

You are so spry and surefooted that it is easy for you to walk on roofs and crawl through small holes."

"There is a river between this village and Duck's-Nest-of-the-Chang-Family," replied the cat. "How can I swim that?"

"You shall ride on my back," said the dog, "and I will swim across."

So the two started out. Soon they came to the river, and the cat stood on the back of the dog while he swam across. When they reached the village of Duck's-Nest-of-the-Chang-Family, the cat said, "Wait here."

Then she climbed up to the top of a wall, and walked along many mud walls till she came to the house of Mr. and Mrs. Chang. They were fast asleep. The cat crept softly through a window, and with the help of a rat, found the place where the golden charm was hidden. She took it in her mouth and hurried back to the dog. When he saw the golden charm in her mouth, he danced around in delight. Then they ran to the riverbank.

"Elder Sister," said the dog, "be careful! You are hungry. Do not open your mouth if you see a fish, or you will drop the golden charm." And this warning he said twice over.

All went well till just as they reached the other bank, a big fish sprang out of the water right under the cat's nose. She gave a leap and snapped her teeth. The golden charm fell out of her mouth and sank to the bottom.

"You lazy, gluttonous beast!" snarled the dog as he sprang upon the bank. "No cat ever kept her mouth shut!"

"You turtle! You rabbit!" hissed the cat.

And while they were thus snarling and hissing, a good-natured frog rose from the water to see what was going on. When he heard about the golden charm, he offered to dive for it. Soon he rose again with it in his mouth. The dog and cat thanked him with many bows, and hastened on to the Widow Wang's house, the cat carrying the golden charm in her teeth.

The door of the little house of rice-straw was fastened, and though the dog barked, no one opened it. At last the cat crawled through the window. The Widow Wang was sitting weeping, while her son sat beside her pale and thin from hunger. The cat leaped down and laid the golden charm at her feet.

The Widow Wang nearly fainted with surprise and joy; then she picked up the golden charm and ran to make a fire. In a second she was crying:

Dumplings, Dumplings, piping hot!
Dumplings, Dumplings, fill the pot!

Then she and her son feasted on a great heap of steaming hot dumplings, more rich and delicious than any they had had before. As for the cat, they smoothed her fur and fed her till her sides stood out.

After the feast was over, the cat slipped into the courtyard where the starving dog was patiently waiting, while he sniffed the fragrant odors of the pork dumplings.

"Oh! Ho! Elder Brother!" laughed the cat. "What big, plump, meat dumplings! You should see how many the Widow Wang fed me! They are all eaten up! Oh! Ho!"

At that the dog gave a great snarl and leaped upon the cat. He seized her and shook her till her teeth rattled.

Ever since then dogs have chased cats, and all cats have been enemies of dogs.

FRANCES JENKINS OLCOTT

≺ Part Three

CUNNING BEASTS AND
TRICKISH MEN

The Man Whose
Trade Was Tricks

There was, there was, and yet there was not, there was once a king who, like all kings, wanted to believe he was the trickiest man in the whole world.

During the day, when his court stood near to applaud each word he spoke, he felt sure of this. But at night when sleep was slow he worried.

Is it possible, is it really possible, he would think to himself, that there might be someone who is trickier than I?

Finally he could endure it no longer, and he called his viziers together.

"Go," he commanded them, "and find the trickiest man in my kingdom and bring him here before me. I will match myself against him. If he loses, he must be my slave for life."

The viziers set out, and in their travels they met many clever men—such clever men, in fact, that they refused to go back and match themselves against the king for no better reward than a promise they might be slaves.

The viziers grew desperate.

At last one night they came through a fertile valley bordered with thick forests into the street of a poor village. Now this village, you should know, was not poor because it was a lazy village or a stupid village. It was poor because the king owned the valley and all the forest beyond. Each year he took such a heavy rent that no matter how hard the villagers worked, when harvest time came nothing was left for them but the middlings of their own wheat and a few crooked tree stumps.

But poor as this village was, they knew how to act like rich men. They called the viziers to the best supper they could cook and afterward, for their entertainment, built a campfire and told stories.

As the evening sharpened itself to a point, the viziers noticed that one man, Shahkro, was better than all the rest at guessing riddles, and remembering poems, and describing his adventures.

"Let us see if he will go with us and match himself against the king," whispered the viziers to each other.

At first when they asked Shahkro he refused, but finally after some persuasion he said, "I will go with you, but I will go just like this. Without my hat and without my cherkasska."

And exactly that way they brought him before the king.

"Sit down," the king said. "So you think you are the trickiest man in my kingdom?"

"Tricking is my trade," Shahkro answered.

"Try to trick me, then," the king commanded. "But I warn

you," he added, "it cannot be done, for I am so tricky myself."

"I can see that," Shahkro said. "I wish I had known all this before. I would have come prepared. As it was I left in such a hurry I didn't stop for my hat or my cherkasska, to say nothing of my tools."

"What tools?"

"Why, the tools I use for tricking people."

"Go and get them."

"That's not so easy. Naturally, as I'm sure you know from your own experience, I can't just bundle them together as though they were something ordinary. I need wagons."

"Wagons?" said the king. "How many wagons?"

"About a hundred, with a hundred horses to pull them."

"Take them from my stable, but come right back."

"Certainly," Shahkro said. "With luck I should have everything loaded in five or six months."

"Five or six months?"

"I'll need to bring *all* my tools if I must trick you."

"Well, come back as soon as you can."

"By the way," Shahkro said, when the wagons were brought and he was ready to drive off, "if I can't trick you I know I must be your slave for the rest of my life, but just suppose I win; what then?"

"But you can't win," the king told him.

"I know I can't, but suppose I did."

"Well, what do you want?"

"Something you wouldn't miss if you gave it to me."

"I agree," said the king.

Shahkro went home at a fast trot, called all the villagers together, gave them each a horse and wagon, and working side by side they sowed and harvested a crop large enough to last them for ten years.

"At least we have this much out of it," Shahkro said, when the last load of grain came creaking into the barn. "Now bring me all the empty wineskins you can find."

When these were collected, Shahkro blew them full of air and piled them on the wagons and rode back to the palace.

The king was waiting impatiently for him in the great hall,

surrounded by all his nobles dressed in their richest costumes.

"Let us begin," the king said.

"I must unpack my tools," Shahkro told him.

"I will send servants to do that," the king said.

While they were waiting, the king's black dog ran into the room and, noticing a stranger was there, he came over and sniffed Shahkro's legs to make his acquaintance.

Shahkro bent his head and blew very lightly in the dog's ear. The dog, of course, in turn licked Shahkro's ear.

"This is awful news," Shahkro jumped up from his chair. "Awful! Where's my hat? Where's my coat? I beg you, loan me the fastest horse in your own stable. My dear wife, whom I left well and happy yesterday, is dying."

"How do you know?" cried the king.

"How does he know?" cried the court.

"Your dog, as you saw, whispered it in my ear just now."

Everyone was sorry, and the king ordered the best horse in his stable saddled, a full-blooded black Arabian, and Shahkro rode away home.

He stayed there long enough to sell the horse for a good price and buy a black donkey.

Then he put the horse's saddle and bridle on the donkey and went back to town.

The king was waiting in the courtyard, and when he saw Shahkro jogging along he cried out, "Where is my horse?"

"Horse?" Shahkro said. "Horse! Oh King, have your joke at my expense. I am only a poor man. But I never thought you would do a thing like this to me. Send me home to my sick wife on a horse that changes himself back and forth to a donkey as it suits his pleasure."

"That's impossible," the king said. "I've had that horse for five years."

"Impossible or not," Shahkro answered. "Here I am the same as I started out for home five days ago. Here is the same bridle in my hands. Here is the same black animal under me. And it's a donkey."

The king looked at the saddle and at the bridle. He ran his hand over the donkey's flank. "Well, all I can say in apology is that he never did it while I rode him. But let's forget all that. When are you going to try to trick me?"

"Right now," Shahkro said. "Sit down. Answer me a question. You claimed you were a trickster. Did you ever use any tools?"

"No."

"Then why did you think I would? So there I tricked you once. In all the years you had your black dog, did he ever talk to you?"

"No."

"Then why did you think he would talk to me? I tricked you twice. In all the years you had your black horse did he ever turn into a donkey for you?"

"No."

"Then why should he for me? There I tricked you three times. Now pay me and I will go."

The king saw he had one last chance to redeem his reputation as a trickster, so he said, "Remember, for your reward I promised only what I wouldn't miss. You must choose something I never use, or otherwise I would miss it. Now what shall it be?"

"Your head," Shahkro answered.

When the king heard this he began to shake and turn so green that Shahkro took pity on him. "Wait," he said, "I will take another reward. Because, on second thought, you do use your head. It keeps your hat from lying on your shoulders. Give me instead your forest and all the fields around it for my village people to use for their own."

"Certainly," said the king, and he called his viziers and sealed the agreement right there and gave it to Shahkro. "And now I don't want to keep you, for I know you are anxious to get home."

Shahkro went back to his village, and in honor he lived there all his life.

As for the king, after that he didn't have to worry any more whether or not he was the trickiest man in the world, so I suppose he slept very well. Or maybe because he was a king he found a new worry to keep him awake.

GEORGE AND HELEN PAPASHVILY

The Fox and the Bear

Long ago, deep, deep in the hills of Japan, there lived a fox and a bear. Neither of them had been able to find much food and both of them were very hungry, so one day the fox came to the bear with a plan.

"I have a good idea, Mr. Bear," the fox said. "Will you listen?"

"Yes, of course," answered the bear. "What is this idea of yours?"

"Well, at the edge of this forest there is a great, wide field," the fox explained. "There is nothing growing in it now, but it could be full of cabbages and onions and good things to eat."

The bear nodded, but he still did not understand. "How?" he asked.

"Why, we'll put them there," the fox went on. "All we need to do is till the soil and plant some seeds. Are you willing to do a little work?"

The bear thought of juicy red carrots and big heads of sweet cabbage, and he could not refuse. "Of course I'll work," he said. "Let's begin right away."

And so the two of them went off to inspect the great, wide field at the edge of the forest. It was full of rocks and weeds that needed to be taken out before anything could be planted.

"Mr. Bear," the fox said as he looked at the land, "you are so much stronger than I, and you have much sharper claws. Will you dig up the land and clear the field while I go home and get some seed?"

So, while the fox went home, the bear got to work. He dug up the tree stumps that were in the middle of the field. He cleared

111

away all the big rocks and he plowed the field in neat, straight rows. When at last he was finished, the fox appeared, carrying a big bag of seed.

"Ah, you have done a fine job, Mr. Bear," he said, looking over the freshly turned soil. "Now, I shall begin my work."

And the fox trotted back and forth, dropping seeds into the soil. Every once in a while, he would stop to rest beneath the shade of a tree saying, "My, this is difficult!" and he would look at the bear to make sure he understood how hard he was working.

When he had finished, he sat down beside the bear. "Well, our planting is done," he said. "Now, all we have to do is wait for the crops to grow. Let's decide who is going to get which half of the crop, so we won't quarrel about it later," the fox suggested.

"All right," the bear agreed. "That's a good idea."

But before he could say anything more, the fox quickly added, "I'll take the half that grows under the soil."

There was nothing left for the bear to say then except, "Very well, I'll take the half that grows on top of the soil."

And so the two agreed to meet again in a few weeks when their crops would be ready to pick, and each went back to his home in the woods.

Before long, tiny green shoots began to appear in even rows over the field, growing bigger and stronger as the days went by. Finally, one day, the fox and the bear decided it was time to harvest their crops and have a feast.

"Look, Mr. Bear," the fox said cheerfully. "You're going to get all that lovely green that's growing on top of the soil."

The bear nodded happily, and lumbered out into the field to pick his half of the crop. As he began to work, the fox called out to him. "Say, Mr. Bear, since you're picking the greens anyway, pull out the roots for me at the same time, will you?"

The bear was so glad to see all the greens, he didn't even mind helping the fox with his half of the crop. While the bear was busy pulling up the crop, the fox was busy cutting off the roots for himself. Soon, he had filled his own baskets full and slipped away quietly. The bear gathered his green leaves in many bundles and then carried them to his cave.

But the next morning, when the bear got up and looked at his greens, he found they had already begun to wither and dry. He tried eating a few, but they were bitter and tasteless.

"I wonder how the fox made out," the bear thought to himself, and he hurried through the forest to visit the fox.

When he got to the fox's home, he saw him lying in the sun, nibbling on a tender, juicy carrot. When he looked inside, he saw that the fox had stored away many, many baskets, all full of tender sweet carrots.

"Were those the roots I dug up for you yesterday?" the bear asked in surprise.

"Why, yes, Mr. Bear," the fox answered without even looking up. "How were your greens?"

"They have already begun to dry, and I couldn't even eat any this morning," the bear said forlornly. Then, looking at all the carrots the fox had, he asked, "Let me have a few of your carrots, Mr. Fox."

But the fox shook his head. "Remember, we made a bargain at the very beginning. You were to get everything that grew on top of the soil, and I was to get everything underneath. A promise is a promise." And the fox wouldn't even give the hungry bear one nibble of his carrot.

A few weeks later, just when the bear had begun to forget about the clever fox, he appeared again in front of the bear's cave.

"I admit I wasn't very fair the last time," he said. "Let's plant another crop, and this time you can choose first which half of the crop you'd like."

The bear wasn't going to be fooled again. "Very well," he said. "This time, I want the half that grows beneath the soil. You take what grows on top."

"Anything you say," the fox answered, and again he trotted away to get the seeds while the bear plowed and dug up the field.

After a few weeks, the bear and the fox met again to look at their crops and found rows and rows of beautiful green leaves.

"Now, Mr. Fox, you take what's on top," the bear said, "and I'll take what's under the ground."

The fox nodded, and quickly got to work picking his crop. When his arms were full, he went home, calling to the bear, "Everything underneath is yours, Mr. Bear."

But when the bear dug up the roots, expecting to find nice tender carrots, all he found were a few thin, scraggly roots about an inch long.

"Why, these aren't carrots!" he thought angrily. "I can't even eat these tiny roots," and he ran to see what the fox had taken home. There he found the fox with several baskets full of beautiful red strawberries. He sat eating them one by one, looking up every once in a while to see if the bear was coming.

"Mr. Fox, you've tricked me again," the bear cried angrily. "Let me at least taste one of your strawberries!"

But the fox shook his head. "You chose the bottom half. You can't have any of the top." And so the bear wandered off sad and hungry.

The bear decided then and there that he would have nothing

more to do with the sly fox, but one day the fox appeared again.

"I have been very wicked," he said, looking very humble. "But let's forget the past and be friends once more. I came today to show you something I know you'll like. Will you come with me?"

"What is it?" the bear asked, for he was going to be very careful this time.

"I've found a beehive full of honey," said the fox, "and I hurried here to tell you because I know how much you like it."

When the bear thought of eating some honey, he could not stay away. He followed the fox into a bamboo thicket where the fox pointed out a beehive in the stump of an old tree.

The bear thought of the sweet, creamy honey inside, and said happily, "Ah, that is truly what I love best." He thanked the fox, and then hurried to the beehive, sniffing all around it to see how he could get the honey. But suddenly, the bees came swarming out of the hive, and buzzing wildly, they stung the poor bear and chased him all the way over the hill, back to his cave in the mountains. The clever fox waited quietly until all the bees had gone after the bear; then he went to the beehive and ate all the honey by himself.

This time the bear really lost his patience. "This is the last time that fox will fool me," he said. "I am going to get my revenge." And he wondered what he might do to punish the wicked fox.

One day, as the bear was eating some horse meat, the fox came strolling up to him. "Good day, Mr. Bear," he said, bowing low. "My, that looks like a good piece of meat. May I have just a little taste?"

The bear suddenly had a good plan. "Go right ahead," he said to the fox. "Take as much as you like."

The fox ate until he was full, and then with a happy sigh, he asked, "Where did you ever find such good horse meat?"

The bear smiled to himself. "It's really very easy, especially for someone your size," he said to the fox.

The fox thought of all the horse meat he could store up for the winter. "Tell me," he said anxiously. "Where do I go? What do I do?"

"Well," the bear went on, "I discovered that just beyond this mountain is a wide meadow beside a cool stream. The meadow is full of green grass, and you will see many, many horses grazing there."

"Yes, yes," the fox said, listening carefully.

"Pick out the biggest horse—the very biggest one you see in the field," the bear went on. "Tie your tail securely to his, and then bite one of his hind legs as hard as you can."

"Is that all?" asked the fox.

The bear nodded. "As soon as you bite the horse's leg, he will weaken and die. Then you'll have all the horse meat you can eat."

The fox hardly waited to thank the bear. He ran as quickly as he could to the big meadow beside the mountain stream. It was green and lovely, and there were many horses grazing there, just as the bear had said. The fox stole quietly behind a big white horse and tied his own tail securely to the horse's. Then he bit one of the hind legs just as hard as he could. The horse gave a terrible cry, kicked up his hind legs, and ran wildly over the field, dragging the fox behind him.

"Help! Stop!" the fox shouted, but the frightened horse just ran all the more. The fox was kicked and dragged over all the stones and stumps that lay in the meadow, and finally thrown against a big tree beside the stream. He was sitting there holding his aching head and moaning to himself when the bear came along to see what had happened.

"Look at me!" the fox whimpered, licking his wounds. "Look what that terrible horse did to me!"

But the bear didn't feel a bit sorry for the fox. "Mr. Fox," he said quietly, "you got exactly what you deserved." And he walked away into the forest without even looking back.

RETOLD BY YOSHIKO UCHIDA

The Magic Cap

There was once a farmer of whom his neighbors used to say that he had no more wits than he was born with, which were not very many. Although it was easy to get the best of him, he was fortunate in having for a wife a woman who was very smart and sharp as a needle. Hence Willem, as he was called, left all of the thinking to his wife and did whatever she told him to do.

One bright, sunny morning she said, "Willem, put on a clean smock and your Sunday clogs and take the cow with you to sell at the market. She is very fat and looks well, so you should get at least a hundred guilders for her."

So to the market went the farmer, pulling the cow behind him.

As he passed a certain inn, three ne'er-do-wells were standing in the doorway.

"There goes Willem, the simpleton," remarked one of them. "It should be easy enough to fool him."

The three put their heads together for an instant and straightaway agreed on a plan to get Willem's cow for little money. Then they took a short cut across the fields and stood here and there along the road where Willem would pass.

As the farmer came toward him, the first scamp called out, "Hi, farmer, are you taking that donkey to market?"

"That is not a donkey; that is a cow," answered Willem.

"Ho, ho! Ha, ha! What kind of a farmer are you to think it is a cow?" And shaking with laughter, the scoundrel walked on.

Shortly afterwards Willem met the second rogue, who said, "Why don't you ride that donkey instead of pulling him, farmer?"

"That is not a donkey; that is a cow," replied Willem again.

117

"A cow? Why, farmer, you must be blind to take that animal for a cow!" And the second scoundrel walked on.

Poor Willem turned around and looked at his cow doubtfully. Had he taken the wrong animal out of the stable? But no, there could be no mistake—this *was* their cow—the one his wife had

told him to take to market. Still, his wife might be wrong too—
they might both be mistaken, and perhaps he *was* leading a donkey, instead of a cow, to market.

Then he met the third scamp. "Good morning, farmer. Is your
donkey for sale?"

There! thought Willem. That was the third person to talk
about a *donkey;* he and his wife *must* be wrong.

"Yes," he finally replied, "I am taking this donkey to
market."

"In that case," said the other, "I will buy it from you for
twenty guilders."

Now, twenty guilders was a good price for a donkey, so
Willem agreed and went back to his farm, well satisfied that he
had made a good sale.

When he got home his wife called him all kinds of an idiot,
until he hung his head in shame. But she knew that it was not
altogether his fault that he had gotten the worst of a bad bargain,
so she put on her thinking cap and tried to find a way to get even
with the three ne'er-do-wells.

Well, just before the next market-day, the farmer's wife arranged to go to town and lay a trap for the three tramps. On
market day itself she gave the farmer an old cap and told him
exactly what he was to do with it.

As Willem was trudging along the road that led to town, he
met the three ne'er-do-wells, who stopped to crow over the trick
they had played on him.

"Oh, let bygones be bygones," said the farmer good-naturedly.
"I have some money to spend today. Will you come and have a
glass of wine with me?"

They gladly accepted and followed him to an inn. After they
had all refreshed themselves, the farmer looked at the innkeeper
and twirling his cap three times upon the forefinger of his right
hand, asked, "Everything is paid for, is it not?"

"Yes, everything is paid for," the innkeeper repeated, as the
farmer walked out, followed by his fair-weather friends.

As they were passing the next inn, Willem stopped and said
aloud, as though talking to himself, "It should work here, too,"

and asking the ne'er-do-wells to join him in another drink, he went inside. And again after they had had their fill, Willem spun his cap around his finger and walked out without paying a cent.

The rogues' eyes were by now fairly popping out of their heads, but no one spoke a word. When they came to the third inn, the farmer said, "Let's have dinner here; it won't cost a thing."

So the four went in and ordered a good dinner. When every one had eaten and drunk his fill, the farmer picked up his cap and twirled it around his finger again, and lo and behold, once more the innkeeper said everything had been paid for!

By that time the three ne'er-do-wells could no longer hold back their curiosity and began questioning Willem. They wanted to know how he could eat and drink in every inn he went to without paying for anything.

The farmer told them that the secret lay in the cap. It was a magic cap, he said.

"How much do you want for your cap?" the first one asked. "I'll give you fifty guilders for it!" he added eagerly.

"I will give you eighty!" the second one cried.

"One hundred!" shouted the third, who was the greediest of all and whose mouth watered when he thought of all the good food and wine he would get if he had the cap in his possession.

"Sold!" said Willem.

The farmer ran all the way home with the hundred guilders in his hand; and how his wife chuckled when he gave her the money! "That's eighty guilders for our loss in the sale of the cow; ten guilders for the food and wine you and your fine friends feasted upon, which I paid for in advance yesterday, when I went to town; and ten guilders to teach those rascals a lesson," she counted, as she put the money in an old stocking and hid it on one of the low wooden beams above her head.

JOHAN HART

The Little Jackal
and the Alligator

The little jackal was very fond of shellfish. He used to go down by the river and hunt along the edges for crabs and such things. And once, when he was hunting for crabs, he was so hungry that he put his paw into the water after a crab without looking first— which you never should do! The minute he put in his paw, *snap!* the big alligator who lives in the mud down there had it in his jaws.

"Oh, dear!" thought the little jackal. "The big alligator has my paw in his mouth! In another minute he will pull me down and gobble me up! What shall I do? what shall I do?" Then he thought, suddenly, "I'll deceive him!"

So he put on a very cheerful voice, as if nothing at all were the matter, and he said, "Ho! ho! Clever Mr. Alligator! Smart Mr. Alligator, to take that old bulrush root for my paw! I hope you'll find it very tender!"

The old alligator was hidden away beneath the mud and bulrush leaves, and he couldn't see anything. He thought, "Pshaw! I've made a mistake." So he opened his mouth and let the little jackal go.

The little jackal ran away as fast as he could, and as he ran he called out, "Thank you, Mr. Alligator! Kind Mr. Alligator! *So* kind of you to let me go!"

The old alligator lashed with his tail and snapped with his jaws, but it was too late; the little jackal was out of reach.

After this the little jackal kept away from the river, out of

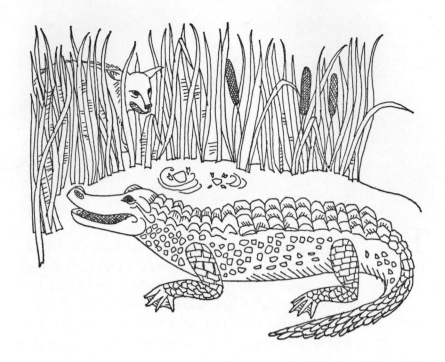

danger. But after about a week he got such an appetite for crabs that nothing else would do at all; he felt that he must have a crab. So he went down by the river and looked all around, very carefully. He didn't see the old alligator, but he thought to himself, "I think I'll not take any chances." So he stood still and began to talk out loud to himself. He said, "When I don't see any little crabs on the land I most generally see them sticking out of the water, and then I put my paw in and catch them. I wonder if there are any fat little crabs in the water today."

The old alligator was hidden down in the mud at the bottom of the river, and when he heard what the little jackal said, he thought, "Aha! I'll pretend to be a little crab, and when he puts his paw in, I'll make my dinner of him." So he stuck the black end of his snout above the water and waited.

The little jackal took one look, and then he said, "Thank you, Mr. Alligator! Kind Mr. Alligator! You are *exceedingly* kind to show me where you are! I will have dinner elsewhere." And he ran away like the wind.

The old alligator foamed at the mouth, he was so angry, but the little jackal was gone.

For two whole weeks the little jackal kept away from the river. Then, one day, he got a feeling inside him that nothing but crabs could satisfy; he felt that he must have at least one crab. Very cautiously, he went down to the river and looked all around. He saw no sign of the old alligator. Still, he did not mean to take any chances. So he stood quite still and began to talk to himself—it was a little way he had. He said, "When I don't see any little crabs on the shore, or sticking up out of the water, I usually see them blowing bubbles from under the water; the little bubbles go *puff, puff, puff,* and then they go *pop, pop, pop,* and they show me where the little juicy crabs are, so I can put my paw in and catch them. I wonder if I shall see any little bubbles today?"

The old alligator, lying low in the mud and weeds, heard this, and he thought, "Pooh! *That's* easy enough; I'll just blow some little crab-bubbles, and then he will put his paw in where I can get it."

So he blew, and he blew, a mighty blast, and the bubbles rose in a perfect whirlpool, fizzing and swirling.

The little jackal didn't have to be told who was underneath those bubbles: he took one quick look, and off he ran. But as he went, he sang, "Thank you, Mr. Alligator! Kind Mr. Alligator! You are the kindest alligator in the world, to show me where you are, so nicely! I'll breakfast at another part of the river."

The old alligator was so furious that he crawled up on the bank and went after the little jackal; but, dear, dear, he couldn't catch the little jackal; he ran far too fast.

After this, the little jackal did not like to risk going near the water, so he ate no more crabs. But he found a garden of wild figs, which were so good that he went there every day, and ate them instead of shellfish.

Now the old alligator found this out, and he made up his mind to have the little jackal for supper or to die trying. So he crept, and crawled, and dragged himself over the ground to the garden of wild figs. There he made a huge pile of figs under the biggest of the wild fig trees, and hid himself in the pile.

After a while the little jackal came dancing into the garden, very happy and carefree—*but* looking all around. He saw the huge pile of figs under the big fig tree.

"H-m," he thought, "that looks singularly like my friend the alligator. I'll investigate a bit."

He stood quite still and began to talk to himself—it was a little way he had. He said, "The little figs I like best are the fat, ripe, juicy ones that drop off when the breeze blows; and then the wind blows them about on the ground, this way and that; the great heap of figs over there is so still that I think they must be all bad figs."

The old alligator, underneath his fig pile, thought, "Bother the suspicious little jackal. I shall have to make these figs roll about so that he will think the wind moves them." And straightway he humped himself up and moved, and sent the little figs flying— and his back showed through.

The little jackal did not wait for a second look. He ran out of the garden like the wind. But as he ran he called back, "Thank you, again, Mr. Alligator; very sweet of you to show me where you are. I can't stay to thank you as I should like: good-bye!"

At this, the old alligator was beside himself with rage. He vowed that he would have the little jackal for supper this time, come what might. So he crept and crawled over the ground till he came to the little jackal's house. Then he crept and crawled inside, and hid himself there in the house, to wait till the little jackal should come home.

By and by the little jackal came dancing home, happy and carefree—*but* looking all around. Presently, as he came along, he saw that the ground was all scratched up as if something very heavy had been dragged over it. The little jackal stopped and looked.

"What's this? what's this?" he said.

Then he saw that the door of his house was crushed at the sides and broken, as if something very big had gone through it.

"What's this? What's this?" the little jackal said. "I think I'll investigate a little!"

So he stood quite still and began to talk to himself (you remember, it was a little way he had), but loudly. He said, "How strange that my little house doesn't speak to me! Why don't you speak to me, Little House? You always speak to me, if everything is all right, when I come home. I wonder if anything is wrong with my little house."

The old alligator thought to himself that he must certainly pretend to be the little house, or the little jackal would never come in. So he put on as pleasant a voice as he could (which is not saying much) and said, "Hullo, Little Jackal!"

Oh! when the little jackal heard that, he was frightened enough, for once.

"It's the old alligator," he said, "and if I don't make an end of him this time he will certainly make an end of me. What shall I do?"

He thought very fast. Then he spoke out pleasantly.

"Thank you, Little House," he said. "It's good to hear your pretty voice, dear Little House, and I will be in with you in a minute; only first I must gather some firewood for dinner."

Then he went and gathered firewood, and more firewood, and more firewood; and he piled it all up solid against the door and round the house; and then he set fire to it!

And it smoked and burned till it smoked that old alligator to smoked herring!

ADAPTED BY SARA CONE BRYANT

The Old Woman
and the Tramp

There was once a tramp who went plodding his way through a forest. The distance between the houses was so great that he had little hope of finding a shelter before the night set in. But all of a sudden he saw some lights between the trees. He then discovered a cottage, where there was a fire burning on the hearth. How nice it would be to roast one's self before that fire, and to get a bite of something, he thought; and so he dragged himself toward the cottage.

Just then an old woman came toward him.

"Good evening, and well met!" said the tramp.

"Good evening," said the woman. "Where do you come from?"

"South of the sun, and east of the moon," said the tramp; "and now I am on the way home again, for I have been all over the world, with the exception of this parish," he said.

"You must be a great traveler, then," said the woman. "What may be your business here?"

"Oh, I want a shelter for the night," he said.

"I thought as much," said the woman; "but you may as well get away from here at once, for my husband is not at home, and my place is not an inn," she said.

"My good woman," said the tramp, "you must not be so cross and hardhearted, for we are both human beings and should help one another, as it is written."

"Help one another?" said the woman, "help? Did you ever hear such a thing? Who'll help me, do you think? I haven't got a morsel in the house! No, you'll have to look for quarters elsewhere," she said.

But the tramp was like the rest of his kind; he did not consider himself beaten at the first rebuff. Although the old woman grumbled and complained as much as she could, he was just as persistent as ever, and went on begging and praying like a starved dog, until at last she gave in, and he got permission to lie on the floor for the night.

That was very kind, he thought, and he thanked her for it.

"Better on the floor without sleep, than suffer cold in the forest deep," he said; for he was a merry fellow, this tramp, and was always ready with a rhyme.

When he came into the room he could see that the woman was not so badly off as she had pretended; but she was a greedy and stingy woman of the worst sort, and was always complaining and grumbling.

He now made himself very agreeable, of course, and asked her in his most insinuating manner for something to eat.

"Where am I to get it from?" said the woman. "I haven't tasted a morsel myself the whole day."

But the tramp was a cunning fellow, he was.

"Poor old granny, you must be starving," he said. "Well, well, I suppose I shall have to ask you to have something with me, then?"

"Have something with you!" said the woman. "You don't look as if you could ask anyone to have anything! What have you got to offer one, I should like to know?"

"He who far and wide does roam, sees many things not known at home; and he who many things has seen, has wits about him and senses keen," said the tramp. "Better dead, than lose one's head! Lend me a pot, granny!"

The old woman now became very inquisitive, as you may guess, and so she let him have a pot.

He filled it with water and put it on the fire, and then he blew with all his might till the fire was burning fiercely all round it. Then he took a four-inch nail from his pocket, turned it three times in his hand, and put it into the pot.

The woman stared with all her might.

"What's this going to be?" she asked.

"Nail broth," said the tramp, and began to stir the water with the porridge stick.

"Nail broth?" asked the woman.

"Yes, nail broth," said the tramp.

The old woman had seen and heard a good deal in her time,

but that anybody could have made broth with a nail, well, she had never heard the like before.

"That's something for poor people to know," she said, "and I should like to learn how to make it."

"That which is not worth having will always go a-begging," said the tramp, but if she wanted to learn how to make it she had only to watch him, he said, and went on stirring the broth.

The old woman squatted on the ground, her hands clasping her knees, and her eyes following his hand as he stirred the broth.

"This generally makes good broth," he said; "but this time it will very likely be rather thin, for I have been making broth the whole week with the same nail. If one only had a handful of sifted oatmeal to put in, that would make it all right," he said. "But what one has to go without, it's no use thinking more about," and so he stirred the broth again.

"Well, I think I have a scrap of flour somewhere," said the old woman, and went out to fetch some, and it was both good and fine.

The tramp began putting the flour into the broth, and went on stirring, while the woman sat staring now at him and then at the pot until her eyes nearly burst their sockets.

"This broth would be good enough for company," he said, putting in one handful of flour after another. "If I had only a bit of salted beef and a few potatoes to put in, it would be fit for gentlefolks, however particular they might be," he said. "But what one has to go without, it's no use thinking more about."

When the old woman really began to think it over, she thought she had some potatoes, and perhaps a bit of beef as well; and these she gave the tramp, who went on stirring, while she sat and stared as hard as ever.

"This will be grand enough for the best in the land," he said.

"Well, I never!" said the woman; "and just fancy—all with a nail!"

He was really a wonderful man, that tramp! He could do more than drink a sup and turn the tankard up, he could.

"If one had only a little barley and a drop of milk, we could ask the King himself to have some of it," he said; "for this is what he has every blessed evening. That I know, for I have been in service under the King's cook," he said.

"Dear me! Ask the King to have some! Well, I never!" exclaimed the woman, slapping her knees. She was quite awestruck at the tramp and his grand connections.

"But what one has to go without, it's no use thinking more about," said the tramp.

And then she remembered she had a little barley; and as for milk, well, she wasn't quite out of that, she said, for her best cow had just calved. And then she went to fetch both the one and the other.

The tramp went on stirring, and the woman sat staring, one moment at him and the next at the pot.

Then all at once the tramp took out the nail.

"Now it's ready, and now we'll have a real good feast," he said. "But to this kind of soup the king and the queen always take a dram or two, and one sandwich at least. And then they always have a cloth on the table when they eat," he said. "But what one has to go without, it's no use thinking more about."

But by this time the old woman herself had begun to feel quite grand and fine, I can tell you; and if that was all that was wanted to make it just as the king had it, she thought it would be nice to have it exactly the same way for once, and play at being king and queen with the tramp. She went straight to a cupboard and brought out the brandy bottle, dram glasses, butter and cheese, smoked beef and veal, until at last the table looked as if it were decked out for company.

Never in her life had the old woman had such a grand feast, and never had she tasted such broth, and just fancy, made only with a nail!

She was in such a good and merry humor at having learned such an economical way of making broth that she did not know how to make enough of the tramp who had taught her such a useful thing.

So they ate and drank, and drank and ate, until they became both tired and sleepy.

The tramp was now going to lie down on the floor. But that would never do, thought the old woman; no, that was impossible. "Such a grand person must have a bed to lie in," she said.

He did not need much pressing. "It's just like the sweet Christmas time," he said, "and a nicer woman I never came across. Ah, well! Happy are they who meet with such good people," said he; and he lay down on the bed and went asleep.

And next morning, when he woke, the first thing he got was coffee and a dram.

When he was going, the old woman gave him a bright dollar piece.

"And thanks, many thanks, for what you have taught me," she said. "Now I shall live in comfort, since I have learned how to make broth with a nail."

"Well, it isn't very difficult if one only has something good to add to it," said the tramp as he went his way.

The woman stood at the door staring after him.

"Such people don't grow on every bush," she said.

G. DJURKLO

How Brother Rabbit Fooled the Whale and the Elephant

One day little Brother Rabbit was running along on the sand, lippety, lippety, when he saw the whale and the elephant talking together. Little Brother Rabbit crouched down and listened to what they were saying. This was what they were saying:

"You are the biggest thing on the land, Brother Elephant," said the whale, "and I am the biggest thing in the sea; if we join together we can rule all the animals in the world, and have our way about everything."

"Very good, very good," trumpeted the elephant. "That suits me; we will do it."

Little Brother Rabbit snickered to himself. "They won't rule me," he said. He ran away and got a very long, very strong rope, and he got his big drum, and hid the drum a long way off in the bushes. Then he went along the beach till he came to the whale.

"Oh, please, dear, strong Mr. Whale," he said, "will you have the great kindness to do me a favor? My cow is stuck in the mud a quarter of a mile from here. And I can't pull her out. But you are so strong and so obliging that I venture to trust you will help me out."

The whale was so pleased with the compliment that he said yes at once.

"Then," said the rabbit, "I will tie this end of my long rope to you, and I will run away and tie the other end round my cow, and when I am ready I will beat my big drum. When you hear that, pull very, very hard, for the cow is stuck very deep in the mud."

"Huh!" grunted the whale, "I'll pull her out, if she is stuck to the horns."

Little Brother Rabbit tied the rope-end to the whale, and ran off, lippety, lippety, till he came to the place where the elephant was.

"Oh, please, mighty and kindly Elephant," he said, making a very low bow, "will you do me a favor?"

"What is it?" asked the elephant.

"My cow is stuck in the mud, about a quarter of a mile from here," said little Brother Rabbit, "and I cannot pull her out. Of course you could. If you will be so very obliging as to help me——"

"Certainly," said the elephant grandly, "certainly."

"Then," said little Brother Rabbit, "I will tie one end of this long rope to your trunk, and the other to my cow, and as soon as I have tied her tightly I will beat my big drum. When you hear that, pull; pull as hard as you can, for my cow is very heavy."

"Never fear," said the elephant, "I could pull twenty cows."

"I am sure you could," said the rabbit politely, "only, be sure to begin gently, and pull harder and harder till you get her."

Then he tied the end of the rope tightly round the elephant's trunk and ran away into the bushes. There he sat down and beat the big drum.

The whale began to pull, and the elephant began to pull, and in a jiffy the rope tightened till it was stretched as hard as could be.

"This is a remarkably heavy cow," said the elephant; "but I'll fetch her!" And he braced his forefeet in the earth and gave a tremendous pull.

"Dear me!" said the whale. "That cow must be stuck mighty tight," and he drove his tail deep in the water and gave a marvelous pull.

He pulled harder; the elephant pulled harder. Pretty soon the whale found himself sliding toward the land. The reason was, of course, that the elephant had something solid to brace against, and, too, as fast as he pulled the rope in a little, he took a turn with it round his trunk!

But when the whale found himself sliding toward the land he was so provoked with the cow that he dove headfirst down to the bottom of the sea. That was a pull! The elephant was jerked off his feet, and came slipping and sliding to the beach, and into the surf. He was terribly angry. He braced himself with all his might and pulled his best. At the jerk, up came the whale out of the water.

"Who is pulling me?" spouted the whale.

"Who is pulling me?" trumpeted the elephant.

And then each saw the rope in the other's hold.

"I'll teach you to play cow!" roared the elephant.

"I'll show you how to fool me!" fumed the whale. And they began to pull again. But this time the rope broke, the whale turned a somersault, and the elephant fell over backwards.

At that, they were both so ashamed that neither would speak to the other. So that broke up the bargain between them.

And little Brother Rabbit sat in the bushes and laughed, and laughed, and laughed.

ADAPTED BY SARA CONE BRYANT

Twigmuntus, Cowbelliantus, Perchnosius

Once upon a time there was a king who was so very learned that no parson in the whole world could surpass him; in fact, he was so learned that ordinary folks could hardly understand what he said, nor could he understand them, either. But in order to have someone to talk with, he procured seven wise professors, who were not quite so learned as himself, but who were just able to interpret his learned sayings so that people could apprehend them, and who could twist and turn about the talk of ordinary folk so that it became sufficiently learned and complicated for the king to understand it.

The king had no son, but he had a daughter, and in order that she should be happily married, and the country governed according to the fundamental principles of his learning, he issued an edict that he who was so learned as to put the king and his professors to silence should have his daughter and half the kingdom there and then. But anyone who attempted the task and did not succeed should lose his head for having dared to exchange words with the king.

That was no joke; but the princess was so fair and beautiful that it was no joke to gaze at her, either. And the king did not keep her caged up, for anyone who wished could see her.

There came princes and counts and barons and parsons and doctors and learned persons from all quarters of the world; and no sooner did they see the princess than they one and all wanted to try their luck. But, however learned they were, their learning never proved sufficient, and every one of them lost his head.

Over in a corner of the kingdom there lived a farmer who had a son. This lad was not stupid; he was quick of apprehension and sharp-witted, and he was not afraid of anything.

When the king's edict came to this out-of-the-way place and the parson had read it from the pulpit, the lad wanted to try his luck. "He who nothing risks, nothing wins," thought the lad; and so he went to the parson and told him that if he would give him lessons in the evenings, he would work for his worship in the daytime, but he wanted to become so learned that he could try a bout with the king and his professors.

"Whoever means to compete with them must be able to do something more than munch bread," said the parson.

"That may be," said the lad; "but I'll try my luck."

The parson thought, of course, that he was mad; but when he could get such a clever hand to work for him only for his keep, he thought he could not very well say no; and so the lad got what he wanted.

He worked for the parson in the daytime, and the parson read with him in the evening; and in this way they went on for some time, but at last the lad grew tired of his books.

"I am not going to sit here and read and grind away, and lose what few wits I have," he said; "and it won't be of much help either, for if you are lucky things will come right of themselves, and if you are not lucky you'll never make a silk purse out of a sow's ear."

And with this he pitched the books on the shelf and went his way.

All at once he came to a large forest, where the trees and the bushes were so thick that it was with difficulty he could get along. While he was thus pushing his way through, he began wondering what he should say when he came to the king's palace, and how best he could make use of the learning he had picked up from the parson. All of a sudden the twig of a tree struck him across his mouth, so that his teeth rattled.

"That is Twigmuntus," he said.

A little while after, he came to a meadow where a cow was standing, bellowing so furiously that it almost deafened him.

"That is Cowbelliantus," he said.

He then came to a river; but as there was neither bridge nor planks across it, he had to put his clothes on his head and swim across.

While he was swimming, a perch came and bit him on the nose.

"That is Perchnosius," he said.

At last he came to the king's palace, where things did not look at all pleasant, for there were men's heads stuck on long stakes round about, and they grinned so horribly that they were enough to frighten anyone out of his wits. But the lad was not easily frightened.

"God's peace!" he said, and raised his cap. "There you stick and grin at me; but who knows if I may not be keeping you company before the day is over, and be grinning with you at others? But if I happen to be alive, you shall not stick there any longer gaping at people," he said.

So he went up to the palace and knocked at the gate.

The guard came out and asked what he wanted.

"I have come to try my luck with the Princess," said the lad.

"You?" said the guard, "well, you're a likely one, you are! Have you lost your senses? There have been princes and counts and barons and parsons and doctors and learned persons here, and all of them have had to pay with their heads for that pleasure; and yet you think you'll succeed!" he said.

"I should say it's no concern of yours," said the lad. "Just open the gate, and you'll see one who's not afraid of anything."

But the guard would not let him in.

"Do as I tell you," said the lad, "or there'll be a fine to-do!"

But the guard would not.

The lad then seized him by the collar and flung him against the wall, so that it creaked; and then he walked straight in to the king, who sat in his parlor with his seven professors about him. Their faces were long and thin, and they looked like puny, sickly

persons about to die. They were sitting with their heads on one side, meditating and staring at the floor.

Then one of them, who looked up, asked the lad in ordinary language, "Who are you?"

"A suitor," said the lad.

"Do you want to try for the Princess's hand?"

"Well, that's about it!" said the lad.

"Have you lost your wits? There have been princes and counts and barons and parsons and doctors and learned persons here, and all of them have gone headless away; so you had better turn about and get away while your head is on your shoulders," he said.

"Don't trouble yourself on that account, but rather think of the head on your own shoulders," said the lad. "You look after yours, and I'll take care of mine! So just begin and let me hear how much wit you have got, for I don't think you look so very clever," he said.

The first professor then began a long harangue of gibberish; and when he had finished the second went on; and then the third; and in this way they continued till at length it was the turn of the seventh. The lad did not understand a single word of it all, but he didn't lose courage, for all that. He only nodded his approval to all of it.

When the last had finished his harangue he asked, "Can you reply to that?"

"That's easy enough," said the lad. "Why, when I was in my cradle and in my go-cart I could twist my mouth about and prate and jabber like you," he said. "But since you are so terribly learned, I'll put a question to you, and that shall not be a long one:

"Twigmuntus, Cowbelliantus, Perchnosius? Can you give me an answer to that?"

And now you should have seen how they stretched their necks and strained their ears. They put on their spectacles and began to look into their books and turn over the leaves.

But while they were searching and meditating, the lad put his hands in his trousers pockets and looked so frank and fearless that they could not help admiring him and wondering that one who was so young could be so learned and yet look just like other people.

"Well, how are you getting on?" said the lad. "Cannot all your learning help you to open your mouths, so that I can have an answer to my question?" he said.

Then they began to ponder and meditate, and then they glanced at the ceiling, and then they stared at the walls, and then they fixed their eyes upon the floor. But they could not give him any answer, nor could the king himself, although he was much more learned than all the others together. They had to give it up, and the lad got the princess and half the kingdom. This he ruled in his own way, and if it did not fare better, it did not fare worse for him than for the king with all his fundamental principles.

G. DJURKLO

The Creation of Man

This is the legend told by North American Indians of how Man was created by the coyote.

The coyote had just finished creating all the inferior animals when he called a council of them together in the forest. "The time has come," he told them, "for the creation of Man."

So the council of animals took their seats in a circle according to their rank, with the lion at the head. Seated next to him was the big grizzly bear, next to him the smaller cinnamon bear, and so on down to the tiny mouse who sat at the lion's left.

It was the lion who spoke first. "Man should be created with a mighty voice like mine," he said, "so that he may roar and frighten away all the animals. Furthermore, he should have long hair covering his body, and sharp claws and terrible fangs."

But the grizzly bear objected. "It's ridiculous for anyone to have a voice like yours! You are always roaring so loudly that you scare away the very prey you wish to capture. I think that Man would be much better off to steal about softly and swiftly without making any noise, and to possess great strength so that he could grasp his prey and hold it."

Then the buck spoke up. "I, too, think it would be very foolish for Man to roar so loudly," he said. "I would prefer to see less attention paid to his throat and more to his ears and eyes. His ears should be like spider webs and his eyes should burn like fire. Also," he added, "to my way of thinking, Man would look very foolish indeed unless he had a magnificent pair of antlers on his head with which to fight his enemies."

But the mountain sheep scoffed at the idea of Man's possessing antlers. "If Man had horns, mostly rolled up, they would give his

head weight and he would therefore have more butting force."

The coyote, who had listened to all this with great impatience, could contain himself no longer.

"I've never heard such stupid speeches in all my life!" he exclaimed. "You are all a pack of noodles and nincompoops! You all want to make Man exactly like yourselves. Why, you might just as well take one of your own cubs and call him Man. As for me, I *know* I'm not the best animal that ever was made. However," he said, drawing himself up boastfully, "Man, of course, would *have* to be created with four legs and five fingers like mine. And as for the lion's voice, well, he could be capable of roaring like a lion but know when not to do so. As for the grizzly bear, Man's feet could be shaped like his to help him to stand erect. And, too, it would be good for Man to be like the grizzly in having no tail, for tails, I have found, are good only for harboring fleas.

"As for our friend the buck, his eyes and ears are pretty good, so Man could be patterned after the buck in that respect. I think, too, that Man should be naked like the fish. I have always envied him his nakedness, for my own hair is a burden to me during most of the year. Therefore, let Man be created without hair. Let him, too, possess claws as long as those of the eagle so that he may be able to hold things in them.

"Finally," he concluded, "with all these attributes Man must certainly be supplied with wits to match my own, for all of you must admit none of you is half so crafty and cunning as I. So in that respect, Man must be just like me."

After this long speech the coyote sat down. But the beaver jumped to his feet immediately. "I never heard such nonsense and twaddle in my life! No tail, indeed! Why, how would he haul mud and sand without one?" And he stated emphatically that Man should have a broad, flat tail like his own.

"You are *all* wrong!" exclaimed the owl. "As for me, I cannot see how Man could be of any use whatsoever without wings."

"Wings? Wings?" shouted the mole. "With wings he would only bump his head against the sky. And if Man had eyes as well as wings, he would get his eyes burnt out by flying too close to the sun. *I* think he should be created without eyes so that he could burrow in the dark, cool earth and be as content with things as I am."

Then the little mouse spoke up in his small, squeaky voice. "*I* think he should have eyes so that he can see what he is eating," he said.

And so, with all the differences of opinion about how Man should be created, the council broke up with all of the animals in an angry, quarrelsome mood. Finally the coyote got in a fight with the beaver and bit a piece out of his cheek. Then the owl flew at the coyote's head and tried to lift up his scalp.

At last, to prove themselves right in their arguments, each of the animals took a lump of earth and started to mold Man as he thought he should be. And each one of them molded a man as nearly like himself as possible, all but the coyote who had his own ideas. But it was so late before they started on their models that darkness fell and they could no longer see to work. So they all lay down and went to sleep.

All, that is, except one! The coyote didn't sleep. He stayed awake and worked on his model all night long. And while all the other animals were sleeping soundly, he crept around softly, pouring water on all the other models. And so all the models were ruined except his own. When the sun crept up over the horizon to bring a new day, the coyote completed his model and gave life to it.

Thus it was that Man was created by the coyote.

RETOLD BY ELIZABETH HOUGH SECHRIST

How Boots Befooled the King

Once upon a time there was a king who was the wisest in all of the world. So wise was he that no one had ever befooled him, which is a rare thing, I can tell you. Now, this king had a daughter who was as pretty as a ripe apple, so that there was no end to the number of the lads who came asking to marry her. Every day there were two or three of them dawdling around the house, so that at last the old king grew tired of having them always about.

So he sent word far and near that whoever should befool him might have the princess and half of the kingdom to boot, for he thought that it would be a wise man indeed who could trick him. But the king also said that whoever should try to befool him and should fail should have a good whipping. This was to keep all foolish fellows away.

The princess was so pretty that there was no lack of lads who came to have a try for her and half of the kingdom, but every one of these went away with a sore back and no luck.

Now, there was a man who was well off in the world and who had three sons; the first was named Peter, and the second was named Paul. Peter and Paul thought themselves as wise as anybody in all of the world, and their father thought as they did.

As for the youngest son, he was named Boots. Nobody thought anything of him except that he was silly, for he did nothing but sit poking in the warm ashes all of the day.

One morning Peter spoke up and said that he was going to the town to have a try at befooling the king, for it would be a fine thing to have a princess in the family. His father did not say no, for if anybody was wise enough to befool the king, Peter was the lad.

So, after Peter had eaten a good breakfast, off he set for the town, right foot foremost. After a while he came to the king's house and—rap! tap! tap!—he knocked at the door.

Well; what did he want?

Oh! he would only like to have a try at befooling the king.

Very good; he should have his try. He was not the first one who had been there that morning, early as it was.

So Peter was shown in to the king.

"Oh, look!" said he. "Yonder are three black geese out in the courtyard!"

But no, the king was not to be fooled so easily as all that. "One goose is enough to look at at a time," said he; "take him away and give him a whipping!"

And so they did, and Peter went home bleating like a sheep.

One day Paul spoke up. "I should like to go and have a try for the princess, too," said he.

Well, his father did not say no, for, after all, Paul was the more clever of the two.

So off Paul went, as merrily as a duck in the rain. By and by he came to the castle, and then he too was brought before the king just as Peter had been.

"Oh, look!" said he, "yonder is a crow sitting in the tree with three white stripes on his back!"

But the king was not so silly as to be fooled in that way. "Here is a Jack," said he, "who will soon have more stripes on his back than he will like. Take him away and give him his whipping!"

Then it was done as the king had said, and Paul went away home bawling like a calf.

One day up spoke Boots. "I should like to go and have a try for the pretty princess, too," said he.

At this they all stared and sniggered. What—he go where his clever brothers had failed and had nothing to show for the trying but a good beating? What had come over the lout! Here was a pretty business, to be sure! That was what they all said.

But all of this rolled away from Boots like water from a duck's back. No matter, he would like to go and have a try like the others. So he begged and begged until his father was glad to let him go to be rid of his teasing, if nothing else.

Then Boots asked if he might have the old tattered hat that hung back of the chimney.

Oh, yes, he might have that if he wanted it, for nobody with good wits was likely to wear such a thing.

So Boots took the hat, and after he had brushed the ashes from his shoes set off for the town, whistling as he went.

The first body whom he met was an old woman with a great load of earthenware pots and crocks on her shoulders.

"Good day, mother," said Boots.

"Good day, son," said she.

"What will you take for all of your pots and crocks?" said Boots.

"Three shillings," said she.

"I will give you five shillings if you will come and stand in front of the King's house and do thus and so when I say this and that," said Boots.

Oh, yes! she would do that willingly enough.

So Boots and the old woman went on together and presently came to the king's house. When they had come there, Boots sat down in front of the door and began bawling as loud as he could —"No, I will not! I will not do it, I say! No, I will not do it!"

So he kept on, bawling louder and louder until he made such a noise that, at last, the king himself came out to see what all of the hubbub was about. But when Boots saw him he only bawled out louder than ever. "No, I will not! I will not do it, I say!"

"Stop! stop!" cried the king, "what is all this about?"

"Why," said Boots, "everybody wants to buy my cap, but I will not sell it! I will not do it, I say!"

"But, why should anybody want to buy such a cap as that?" said the king.

"Because," said Boots, "it is a fooling cap and the only one in all of the world."

"A fooling cap!" said the king. For he did not like to hear of such a cap as that coming into the town. "Hum-m-m-m! I should like to see you fool somebody with it. Could you fool that old body yonder with the pots and the crocks?"

"Oh, yes! that is easily enough done," said Boots, and without more ado he took off his tattered cap and blew into it. Then he put it on his head again and bawled out, "Break pots! break pots!"

No sooner had he spoken these words than the old woman jumped up and began breaking and smashing her pots and crocks as though she had gone crazy. That was what Boots had paid her five shillings for doing, but of it the king knew nothing. "Hui!" said he to himself, "I must buy that hat from the fellow or he will fool the princess away from me for sure and certain." Then he began talking to Boots as sweetly as though he had honey in his mouth. Perhaps Boots would sell the hat to him?

Oh, no! Boots could not think of such a thing as selling his fooling cap.

Come, come; the king wanted that hat, and sooner than miss buying it he would give a whole bag of gold money for it.

At this Boots looked up and looked down, scratching his head. Well, he supposed he would have to sell the hat sometime, and the king might as well have it as anybody else. But for all that he did not like parting with it.

So the king gave Boots the bag of gold, and Boots gave the king the old tattered hat, and then he went his way.

After Boots had gone the king blew into the hat and blew into the hat, but though he blew enough breath into it to sail a big ship, he did not befool so much as a single titmouse. Then, at last, he began to see that the fooling cap was good on nobody else's head but Boots's; and he was none too pleased at that, you may be sure.

As for Boots, with his bag of gold he bought the finest clothes that were to be had in the town, and when the next morning had come he started away bright and early for the king's house. "I have come," said he, "to marry the princess, if you please."

At this the king hemmed and hawed and scratched his head. Yes; Boots had befooled him sure enough, but, after all, he could not give up the princess for such a thing as that. Still, he would give Boots another chance. Now, there was the high-councilor, who was the wisest man in all of the world. Did Boots think that he could fool him also?

Oh, yes! Boots thought that it might be done.

Very well; if he could befool the high-councilor so as to bring him to the castle the next morning against his will, Boots should have the princess and the half of the kingdom; if he did not do so he should have his beating.

Then Boots went away, and the king thought that he was rid of him now for good and all.

As for the high-councilor, he was not pleased with the matter at all, for he did not like the thought of being fooled by a clever rogue and taken here and there against his will. So when he had come home, he armed all of his servants with blunderbusses, and then waited to give Boots a welcome when he should come.

But Boots was not going to fall into any such trap as that! No indeed! Not he! The next morning he went quietly and bought a fine large meal sack. Then he put a black wig over his beautiful red hair, so that no one might know him. After that he went to the place where the high-councilor lived, and when he had come there he crawled inside of the sack and lay just beside the door of the house.

By and by came one of the maidservants to the door, and there lay the great meal sack with somebody in it.

"Ach!" cried she, "who is there?"

But Boots only said, "Sh-h-h-h-h!"

Then the serving maid went back into the house, and told the high-councilor that one lay outside in a great meal sack, and that all that he said was, "Sh-h-h-h-h!"

So the councilor went himself to see what it was all about. "What do you want here?" said he.

"Sh-h-h-h-h!" said Boots. "I am not to be talked to now. This is a wisdom sack, and I am learning wisdom as fast as a drake can eat peas."

"And what wisdom have you learned?" said the councilor.

Oh! Boots had learned wisdom about everything in the world. He had learned that the clever scamp who had fooled the king yesterday was coming with seventeen tall men to take the high-councilor, willy-nilly, to the castle that morning.

When the high-councilor heard this he fell to trembling till his teeth rattled in his head. "And have you learned how I can get the better of this clever scamp?" said he.

Oh, yes! Boots had learned that easily enough.

So, good! Then if the wise man in the sack would tell the high-councilor how to escape the clever rogue, the high-councilor would give the wise man twenty dollars.

But no, that was not to be done; wisdom was not bought so cheaply as the high-councilor seemed to think.

Well, the councilor would give him a hundred dollars, then.

That was good! A hundred dollars were a hundred dollars. If the councilor would give him that much he might get into the sack himself, and then he could learn all the wisdom that he wanted, and more besides.

So Boots crawled out of the sack, and the councilor paid his hundred dollars and crawled in.

As soon as he was in all snug and safe, Boots drew the mouth of the sack together and tied it tightly. Then he flung sack, councilor, and all over his shoulder, and started away to the king's house, and anybody who met them could see with half an eye that the councilor was going against his will.

When Boots came to the king's castle he laid the councilor down in the goose-house, and then he went to the king.

When the king saw Boots again, he bit his lips with vexation. "Well," said he, "have you fooled the councilor?"

"Oh, yes!" says Boots, "I have done that."

And where was the councilor now?

Oh, Boots had just left him down in the goose-house. He was tied up safe and sound in a sack, waiting till the king should send for him.

So the councilor was sent for, and when he came the king saw at once that he had been brought against his will.

"And now may I marry the princess?" said Boots.

But the king was not willing for him to marry the princess yet; no! no! Boots must not go so fast. There was more to be done yet. If he would come tomorrow morning he might have the princess and welcome, but he would have to pick her out from among fourscore other maids just like her; did he think that he could do that?

Oh, yes! Boots thought that that might be easy enough to do.

So, good! then come tomorrow; but he must understand that if he failed he should have a good whipping and be sent packing from the town.

So off went Boots, and the king thought that he was rid of him now, for he had never seen the princess, and how could he pick her out from among eighty others?

But Boots was not going to give up so easily as all that! No, not he! He made a little box, and then he hunted up and down until he had caught a live mouse to put into it.

When the next morning came he started away to the king's house, taking his mouse along with him in the box.

There was the king, standing in the doorway, looking out into the street. When he saw Boots coming toward him he made a wry face. "What!" said he, "are you back again?"

Oh, yes! Boots was back again. And now if the princess was ready he would like to go and find her, for lost time was not to be gathered again like fallen apples.

So off they marched to a great room, and there stood eighty-and-one maidens, all as much alike as peas in the same dish.

Boots looked here and there, but, even if he had known the princess, he could not have told her from the others. But he was ready for all that. Before anyone knew what he was about, he opened the box, and out ran the little mouse among them all. Then what a screaming and a hubbub there was. Many looked as though they would have liked to swoon, but only one of them did so. As soon as the others saw what had happened, they forgot all about the mouse, and ran to her and fell to fanning her and slapping her hands and chafing her temples.

"This is the princess," said Boots.

And so it was.

After that the king could think of nothing more to set Boots to do, so he let him marry the princess as he had promised, and have half of the kingdom to boot.

That is all of this story.

Only this: It is not always the silliest one that sits kicking his feet in the ashes at home.

HOWARD PYLE

≺ *Part Four*
STRANGE HAPPENINGS

Schippeitaro

Once upon a time long, long ago, when fairies, giants, ogres and dragons lived on the earth, a brave young warrior set forth in search of adventure.

His way led through a thick forest, and when he finally emerged just at dusk he found himself on a deserted mountainside. He looked all around, hoping to catch sight of a village, or of even one lonely cottage that might be on the edge of the woods. But not a sign of life could he see, and he felt himself to be hopelessly lost.

The path he had been following was so overgrown with briars that after wandering around trying to see some sign of habitation, he even lost track of that. Night was fast approaching, and already the darkness made the trees cast strange and eerie shadows. He was weary and very hungry, but he made himself press on, hoping to find some sort of shelter to protect him from the chilly dews. At last he came upon a deserted temple, and although it was in ruins he was grateful to have found some place where he could spend the night. Thankfully, he wrapped his mantle around him, and making sure his trusty sword was within reach, he lay down and before long was in a deep sleep.

Just at midnight he was awakened by a terrible noise. At first, being half asleep, he thought he must have been having a dream, but the noise continued and he knew it was real. The whole place was resounding with bloodcurdling shrieks and yells.

Grasping his sword, the young warrior got cautiously to his feet and looked through a hole in the wall. There outside the temple in the bright moonlight he beheld a strange and terrifying sight. Squealing and yowling and engaged in a wild and horrible

156

dance was a group of the most hideous cats imaginable. Their terrible yells made the whole mountainside echo.

While the young warrior watched this gruesome sight in horror and amazement, he was suddenly aware that in the midst of their unearthly cries he could distinguish these words:

> *All we fear is Schippeitaro;*
> *We dread to hear his bark.*
> *All we fear is Schippeitaro;*
> *Let's keep our secret dark.*

Then, as suddenly as they had appeared, the phantom cats disappeared, and again all was silent. The young warrior lay down once more, and this time he slept soundly until morning. Eager to leave the scene of his night's adventure, he was happy in the daylight to find the path he had wandered from the evening before. To his great joy it eventually led him to a little village.

Hoping to find food, for by this time he was exceedingly hungry, he was making his way toward the nearest cottage when he heard a woman's voice raised in loud cries and lamentations. He hurried on, his hunger forgotten, to find out her trouble and to see if he could help her in any way.

Standing near the doorway to her cottage was a group of people looking very sorrowful. The young knight questioned them as to why the woman was weeping and asked if there was any way he could aid her. They all shook their heads sadly.

"No," said one. "There is naught you can do. Every year the Spirit of the Mountain devours a victim. Each time he chooses the village's loveliest maiden, and tonight he will claim her. That is the maiden's mother, who is grieving over the fate that will befall her daughter."

On questioning further, the warrior learned that the girl would be placed in a cage and carried to a ruined temple and left there. Each year the pattern was the same. In the morning the victim would have vanished, and there was nothing to be done.

As the warrior talked with the villagers about the girl's tragic fate, he realized that the temple was the same one where he had spent the previous night. He was filled with a desire to help the maiden, and suddenly he was reminded of the phantom cats.

"Have you ever heard the name Schippeitaro?" he asked.

"Of course," one youth replied. "That is the name of a strong and beautiful dog. He belongs to the head man of our prince. I have often seen Schippeitaro with his master, and he looks fine and brave."

The soldier thanked the youth and then hurried off to find Schippeitaro's master. He begged the man to let him have Schippeitaro for just one night. The man was reluctant to lend the dog, but when the young soldier promised faithfully to return him the next morning, the dog's master finally consented, and the warrior led Schippeitaro away.

Then he went back to the cottage where the young girl was awaiting her fate. He told her parents to conceal their daughter in the house and to guard her carefully until his return. Thereupon he placed Schippeitaro in the cage which had been prepared for the maiden. He asked some of the young men of the village to help him carry the cage to the ruined temple. Although he urged them to wait with him they couldn't be persuaded. They were so anxious to leave the haunted spot that they ran down the mountain as though the hobgoblin spirit were right at their heels!

So the young warrior with only Schippeitaro, the dog, for company waited for night to come. Close to midnight he hid in the temple so he would not be observed when the cats returned. At precisely midnight, just as it had befallen the evening before, the phantom cats appeared. This time in their midst was a huge tomcat, so fierce and horrible that the knight knew it was the arch fiend himself. The monster looked all around, and when he spied the cage he danced all around it, yowling with sounds of triumph. His companions, all making the same chilling sounds, followed him. If the maiden had been in the cage she surely would have swooned at the terrible sight. Then the tomcat rushed upon the cage and tore open the door.

But this time he had met his match. With one great lunge Schippeitaro sprang upon him, and seizing him with his teeth, held him fast. The young warrior leaped forward and with one stroke of his sword laid the monster dead at his feet.

The other cats, too stunned to run away, stood gazing at the dead body of their leader. It took just about a minute for the warrior and Schippeitaro to get rid of them, too.

When the young soldier brought Schippeitaro back to his master he was greeted by all the people of the village, rejoicing that the fiend had claimed his last victim. The parents of the girl thanked him a thousand times over for what he had done for them. But the warrior would only say, "You owe it all to Schippeitaro." And then, after bidding them farewell, he set forth on his way to seek new adventures.

Retold by Janette Woolsey

The Maiden with
the Black Wooden Bowl

In the olden days in Japan, there lived a couple who had an only child, a daughter. This maiden was blessed with great charm and remarkable beauty. But even though she won the admiration of all who beheld her, she was not proud. She worked hard in the rice fields along with her mother and father.

When her father died, her mother, believing that she, too, had not long to live, called her daughter to her.

"My child," she said, "you know that you have great beauty, and the thought of leaving you alone in the world frightens me. I have finally decided on a way to protect you from anyone who might wish to do you harm after I am gone."

The maid wept when her mother spoke of leaving her, but her mother bade her dry her tears and listen to what she had to say.

"Fetch me that black wooden bowl," she told her daughter.

When the maiden did as her mother had requested, the mother took the bowl and placed it over her daughter's head so that it completely concealed the beauty of the young girl's face.

"Always wear this, my child, and promise me that you will not remove it until the right time."

"But how shall I know the right time?" the young girl asked. "And besides, the bowl is heavy and uncomfortable."

"You will know," her mother answered. "Now grant me this last request so I can depart this world in peace."

"I promise," the maiden told her mother. "I promise anything you ask."

Not very long after that, the mother died and the young maiden went out into the world to earn her living working in the rice fields. It was hard and weary work, and she had to toil from early morning until evening. Besides this, she had to endure the taunts of her fellow workers, who made fun of her. They even tried to pry the bowl off her head, but when they touched it, it was

as though they had thrust their hands into a bush of nettles. This made the poor girl more unpopular than ever, and the workers constantly complained of her to their employer. As a result, she was forced to seek work in one place after another. Indeed, she traveled about so much that she became known throughout the land as "the maiden with the black wooden bowl."

At last the poor girl found employment in the rice fields of a rich farmer. This man observed how diligently she worked and with what patience she endured the unkind remarks of her fellow workers. He was so impressed, in fact, that when his wife became ill he asked the maid to live in their house and nurse her. The girl gratefully accepted and tended the farmer's wife with the utmost care. The farmer and his wife grew very fond of the girl, and even though their relatives and friends made unkind and spiteful remarks, they treated her as their daughter.

When she had been living with them for several months, their son, who had been studying in Kyoto, came home for a visit. Of course he noticed the girl with the black bowl on her head the first thing.

"Who is this maiden living in our house?" he demanded. "And why does she wear that black bowl?"

His father told him her sad story and the young man found himself becoming more and more interested in the maiden. Indeed, as he got to know her better and observed how charming and gentle she was, his interest began to turn into love and he resolved to marry her.

But when he asked the maiden to be his wife she refused.

"No," she said. "I cannot marry you. I am really nothing more than a servant in your parents' home. And besides, I am such an object of ridicule that you soon would become the laughingstock of all your friends and relatives."

The young man would not accept this answer and pleaded his case with such eloquence that at last the maid consented.

Although all the villagers thought the young man was out of his mind, not one refused an invitation to the wedding. They were all too curious to want to miss what they thought would be a strange ceremony.

As was the custom, when the time came for the bride to be arrayed in her wedding finery, the young maidens of the village came to help her. They had brought with them a fine gown of brocaded satin and a cloak embroidered in gold to hang around her shoulders.

"Now it's time to remove the bowl," they cried. "We want to

arrange your hair with these beautiful combs we have brought as our gift to you."

Then the maiden remembered that her mother had told her she would know when the time had come for her to remove the bowl. "This is the time," she thought.

So she told the maidens to remove it. But, tug as hard as they could, the bowl remained firmly fixed on the young girl's head. She herself tried, too, but the bowl just wouldn't move.

And so she was led into the presence of the bridegroom with the bowl as it had been for so long. The poor girl was so ashamed she wanted to release the young man from his promise to marry her.

"Do not be troubled," he said. "I love you with the bowl as much as I could possibly love you without it." And he ordered the marriage ceremony to proceed.

At that moment there was a loud noise and the bowl burst apart. As it did, the young maiden was showered with silver, gold and jewels of every kind: diamonds, rubies, pearls and emeralds.

The guests gasped in astonishment when they beheld the jewels and then the radiant beauty of the bride. But the bridegroom paid no attention to the jewels. He could see nothing but his bride's face.

"My dear," he whispered, "there are no jewels in the world that can compare with the beauty of your eyes."

RETOLD BY JANETTE WOOLSEY

Tom Tit Tot

Once upon a time there was a woman, and she baked five pies. And when they came out of the oven, they were that overbaked the crusts were too hard to eat. So she says to her daughter, "Darter," says she, "put you them there pies on the shelf, and leave 'em there a little, and they'll come again." She meant, you know, the crust would get soft.

But the girl, she says to herself, "Well, if they'll come again, I'll eat 'em now." And she set to work and ate 'em all, first and last.

Well, come suppertime the woman said, "Go you, and get one o' them there pies. I dare say they've come again now."

The girl went and she looked, and there was nothing but the dishes. So back she came and says she, "Noo, they ain't come again."

"Not one of 'em?" says the mother.

"Not one of 'em," says she.

"Well, come again, or not come again," said the woman, "I'll have one for supper."

"But you can't, if they ain't come," said the girl.

"But I can," says she. "Go you, and bring the best of 'em."

"Best or worst," says the girl, "I've ate 'em all, and you can't have one till that's come again."

Well, the woman she was done, and she took her spinning to the door to spin, and as she span she sang:

> *My darter ha' ate five, five pies today.*
> *My darter ha' ate five, five pies today.*

The king was coming down the street, and he heard her sing, but what she sang he couldn't hear, so he stopped and said, "What was that you were singing, my good woman?"

The woman was ashamed to let him hear what her daughter had been doing, so she sang, instead of that:

> *My darter ha' spun five, five skeins today.*
> *My darter ha' spun five, five skeins today.*

"Stars o' mine!" said the king, "I never heard tell of anyone that could do that."

Then he said, "Look you here, I want a wife, and I'll marry your daughter. But look you here," says he, "eleven months out of the year she shall have all she likes to eat, and all the gowns she likes to get, and all the company she likes to keep; but the last month of the year she'll have to spin five skeins every day, and if she don't I shall kill her."

"All right," says the woman; for she thought what a grand marriage that was. And as for the five skeins, when the time came, there'd be plenty of ways of getting out of it, and likeliest, he'd have forgotten all about it.

Well, so they were married. And for eleven months the girl had all she liked to eat, and all the gowns she liked to get, and all the company she liked to keep.

But when the time was getting over, she began to think about the skeins and to wonder if he had 'em in mind. But not one word did he say about 'em, and she thought he'd wholly forgotten 'em.

However, the last day of the last month he takes her to a room she'd never set eyes on before. There was nothing in it but a spinning wheel and a stool. And says he, "Now, my dear, here you'll be shut in tomorrow with some victuals and some flax, and if you haven't spun five skeins by the night, your head'll go off."

And away he went about his business.

Well, she was that frightened, she'd always been such a gatless girl, that she didn't so much as know how to spin, and what was she to do tomorrow with no one to come nigh her to help her? She sat down on a stool in the kitchen, and law! how she did cry!

However, all of a sudden she heard a sort of a knocking low down on the door. She upped and oped it, and what should she see but a small little black thing with a long tail. That looked up at her right curious, and that said, "What are you a-crying for?"

"What's that to you?" says she.

"Never you mind," that said, "but tell me what you're a-crying for."

"That won't do me no good if I do," says she.

"You don't know that," that said, and twirled that's tail round.

"Well," says she, "that won't do no harm, if that don't do no good," and she upped and told about the pies, and the skeins, and everything.

"This is what I'll do," says the little black thing, "I'll come to your window every morning and take the flax and bring it spun at night."

"What's your pay?" says she.

That looked out of the corner of that's eyes, and that said: "I'll give you three guesses every night to guess my name, and if

you haven't guessed it before the month's up you shall be mine."

Well, she thought she'd be sure to guess that's name before the month was up. "All right," says she, "I agree."

"All right," that says, and law! how that twirled that's tail.

Well, the next day, her husband took her into the room, and there was the flax and the day's food.

"Now, there's the flax," says he, "and if that ain't spun up this night, off goes your head." And then he went out and locked the door.

He'd hardly gone, when there was a knocking against the window.

She upped and she oped it, and there sure enough was the little old thing sitting on the ledge.

"Where's the flax?" says he.

"Here it be," says she. And she gave it to him.

Well, come the evening a knocking came again to the window. She upped and she oped it, and there was the little old thing with five skeins of flax on his arm.

"Here it be," says he, and he gave it to her.

"Now, what's my name?" says he.

"What, is that Bill?" says she.

"Noo, that ain't," says he, and he twirled his tail.

"Is that Ned?" says she.

"Noo, that ain't," says he, and he twirled his tail.

"Well, is that Mark?" says she.

"Noo, that ain't," says he, and he twirled his tail harder, and away he flew.

Well, when her husband came in, there were the five skeins ready for him. "I see I shan't have to kill you tonight, my dear," says he; "you'll have your food and your flax in the morning," says he, and away he goes.

Well, every day the flax and the food were brought, and every day that there little black impet used to come mornings and evenings. And all the day the girl sate trying to think of names to say to it when it came at night. But she never hit on the right one. And as it got towards the end of the month, the impet began to look so maliceful, and that twirled that's tail faster and faster each time she gave a guess.

At last it came to the last day but one. The impet came at night along with the five skeins, and that said, "What, ain't you got my name yet?"

"Is that Nicodemus?" says she.

"Noo, 'tain't," that says.

"Is that Sammle?" says she.

"Noo, 'tain't," that says.

"A-well, is that Methusalem?" says she.

"Noo, 'tain't that neither," that says.

Then that looks at her with that's eyes like a coal o' fire, and that says, "Woman, there's only tomorrow night, and then you'll be mine!" And away it flew.

Well, she felt that horrid. However, she heard the king coming along the passage. In he came, and when he sees the five skeins, he says, says he, "Well, my dear," says he. "I don't see but what you'll have your skeins ready tomorrow night as well, and as I reckon I shan't have to kill you, I'll have supper in here tonight." So they brought supper, and another stool for him, and down the two sate.

Well, he hadn't eaten but a mouthful or so when he stops and begins to laugh.

"What is it?" says she.

"A-why," says he, "I was out a-hunting today, and I got away to a place in the wood I'd never seen before. And there was an old chalk-pit. And I heard a kind of a sort of humming. So I got off my hobby, and I went right quiet to the pit, and I looked down. Well, what should there be but the funniest little black thing you ever set eyes on. And what was that doing, but that had a little spinning wheel, and that was spinning wonderful fast, and twirling that's tail. And as that span that sang:

> *" 'Nimmy nimmy not*
> *My name's Tom Tit Tot.' "*

Well, when the girl heard this, she felt as if she could have jumped out of her skin for joy, but she didn't say a word.

Next day that there little thing looked so maliceful when he came for the flax. And when night came she heard that knocking against the windowpanes. She oped the window, and that come right in on the ledge. That was grinning from ear to ear, and oo! that's tail was twirling round so fast.

"What's my name?" that says, as that gave her the skeins.

"Is that Solomon?" she says, pretending to be afeard.

"Noo, 'tain't," that says, and that came farther into the room.

"Well, is that Zebedee?" says she again.

"Noo, 'tain't," says the impet. And then that laughed and twirled that's tail till you couldn't hardly see it.

"Take time, woman," that says; "next guess, and you're mine." And that stretched out that's black hands at her.

Well, she backed a step or two, and she looked at it, and then she laughed out, and says she, pointing her finger at it:

Nimmy nimmy not
Your name's Tom Tit Tot.

Well, when that heard her, that gave an awful shriek and away that flew into the dark, and she never saw it any more.

JOSEPH JACOBS

The Golden Boat

Once there was a youth who lived with his aunt. She was a very mean and dishonest woman. The youth was always such a good boy that his aunt thought he was stupid. She wanted to make him leave home and never return. Every day she sent him to a swamp to catch frogs and told him not to come back until his basket was full. But his basket always was full, so she found no excuse for driving him away.

One morning as he went to the swamp to catch frogs, he saw a bag of money lying beside the path. He did not know whose it was, so he sat down and watched over it. He hoped that the owner would return for it. Toward evening he saw a man looking here and there along the path. "Have you lost anything?" asked the boy.

"Yes, a bag of money," said the man, who looked very worried.

"I found it, and here it is," said the youth.

The man was so happy to get all his money back that he said, "I will give you half of this."

The youth replied, "I do not want a reward. I have done only my duty."

When he returned home, his aunt saw his empty basket. She thought to herself, "Now I have an excuse for driving this stupid boy from home." So she cried out, "How dare you return with an empty basket?"

The boy told her what had happened. "You are even more stupid than I thought," she shrieked at him. "Take your basket and stick, and go. And don't ever let me see your face again!" And she drove him away.

It was the night of the Moon Festival, and the moon was big and bright. As the youth walked along he wondered where he would go. He looked up at the full moon and recalled what he had often heard. That on the night of the Moon Festival, he who looks long at the moon may see some beautiful object floating down toward him. And that object always brings good luck. The youth gazed and gazed at the heavenly mirror. At last he saw a tiny golden boat floating down on a silver moonbeam. Little people were rowing the boat. Some were playing musical instruments; some were singing; some were dancing.

With a shout of joy the youth held out his basket and cried, "Heavenly boat! Heavenly boat! Drop into my basket!"

One of the musicians bowed and said, "Because you are so kind and so honest, we have come to help you." Then he went into the golden boat, and all the other little people followed him.

The door closed behind them, and the golden boat became smaller and smaller and fell into the basket.

The happy youth walked on with his treasure. At last he came to the city of the emperor. Here he heard of a princess who was both beautiful and good. Hoping to catch sight of her, he went to the palace and found work as a servant.

Sometimes when he was tired he took the little boat from the treasure bag which hung from his waist and looked at it. Sometimes he cried out, "Heavenly ones, heavenly ones, come and play for me!" Then the tiny beings stepped out upon the deck and played, sang, and danced for him.

The emperor heard of the golden boat. He commanded that the owner bring it to him. When the youth stood before the dragon throne, he held the tiny boat in his two hands and cried, "Heavenly ones, heavenly ones, come and play for me."

Out stepped the little people and began to entertain the emperor. He was delighted and longed to have it for his own. He promised the youth his daughter in marriage if he would give him the golden boat. The youth gave it to him, but the emperor had no thought of carrying out his promise. That wicked man had the youth taken to the house of the Demon with the Red Face

and the Demon with the Green Face. The emperor well knew that no man had ever spent a night in that house and lived.

At midnight the Demon with the Red Face and the Demon with the Green Face burst into the house. Their long noses twitched as they sniffed about in the dark. Red Face cried, "Some one has dared to enter our house!"

"Yes! And here he is!" cried Green Face, who leaned over the youth, who was sleeping quietly in the moonlight with a happy smile upon his face.

Red Face gasped and cried, "A blue lotus youth. How beautiful he is!"

"He must be from heaven!" murmured Green Face.

The youth woke and opened his eyes. He smiled up at the two demons and asked, "Have you come at the command of the Emperor?"

They shook their heads. Green Face asked, "Are you a being of heaven or of earth?"

The youth smiled and answered, "I am of earth."

"Do you not fear me?" shouted Green Face.

"Do you not fear me?" shouted Red Face.

The youth looked puzzled and asked, "Fear you? Why should I fear you? Do you fear me?"

At this the demons gasped with surprise. They looked at each other, and burst into laughter that made the roof tiles dance. At last Green Face said, "Blue Lotus Youth, we will give this house to you. We will show you where all our treasures are hidden. They too shall be yours."

The next morning when the officers of the emperor came to the house of the Demon of the Red Face and the Demon of the Green Face, they expected to find the youth dead. Imagine their surprise when he came to meet them clad in beautiful embroidered robes. He said, "Send your servants here. I have gifts which I wish to take to the palace."

Blue Lotus Youth took some of the treasures to the emperor, who was surprised, for they were more precious than anything in the palace. He saw that the youth was so good and honest that he did not suspect him of evil. Even the demons had been kind to him. This filled the emperor with shame, and he welcomed the youth to the palace and gave him for his wife the princess who was both beautiful and good.

Happy indeed were the young bride and groom. And the goodness of the youth shone like a white light through the lantern of his face. Little by little the cruelty and dishonesty of the emperor changed to kindness and honesty. Thus, all unknowing, Blue Lotus Youth became a great power for good in the empire.

One day the youth said to the princess who was his wife, "I shall send to my aunt enough money so that she may live in comfort all her life." And with the bag of money, he sent a note thanking her for her kindness in sending him forth into the world, and thus helping him to find happiness.

BERTA METZGER

The Conjure Wives

Once upon a time when a Halloween night came on the dark o' the moon, a lot o' old conjure wives was a-sittin' by the fire an' a-cookin' a big supper for theirselves.

The wind was a-howlin' round like it does on Halloween nights, an' the old conjure wives they hitched theirselves up to the fire an' talked about the spells they was a-goin' to weave long come midnight.

By an' by there come a knockin' at the door.

"Who's there?" called an old conjure wife. "Who-o? Who-o?"

"One who is hungry and cold," said a voice.

Then the old conjure wives, they all burst out laughin' an' they called out,

> We's a-cookin' for ourselves.
> Who'll cook for you?
> Who? Who?

The voice didn't say nothin', but the knockin' just kept on.

"Who's that a-knockin'?" called out another conjure wife. "Who? Who?"

Then there come a whistlin', wailin' sound:

> Let me in, do-o-o-o!
> I'se cold thro-o-o-o,
> An' I'se hungry too-o-o!

Then the old conjure wives, they all burst out laughin', an' they commenced to sing out:

176

Git along, do!
We's a-cookin' for ourselves.
Who'll cook for you?
Who? Who?

The voice didn't say nothin', but the knockin' just kept on.

Then the old conjure wives they went to work a-cookin' of the supper for theirselves, an' the voice didn't say nothin', but the knockin' just kept on.

An' then the old conjure wives they hitched up to the fire an' they ate an' they ate—an' the voice didn't say nothin', but the knockin' just kept on. An' the old conjure wives they called out again:

Go away, do!
We's a-cookin' for ourselves.
Who'll cook for you?
Who? Who?

An' the voice didn't say nothin', but the knockin' just kept on.

Then the old conjure wives began to get scared-like, an' one of 'em says, "Let's give it somethin' an' get it away before it spoils our spells."

An' the voice didn't say nothin', but the knockin' just kept on.

Then the old conjure wives they took the littlest piece of dough, as big as a pea, an' they put it in the fry pan.

An' the voice didn't say nothin', but the knockin' just kept on.

An' when they put the dough in the fry pan it begun to swell an' swell, an' it swelled over the fry pan an' it swelled over the top o' the stove an' it swelled out on the floor.

An' the voice didn't say nothin', but the knockin' just kept on.

Then the old conjure wives got scared an' they ran for the door, an' the door was *shut tight*.

An' the voice didn't say nothin', but the knockin' just kept on.

An' then the dough it swelled an' it swelled an' it swelled all over the floor an' it swelled up into the chairs. An' the old conjure wives they climbed up on the backs of the chairs an' they were scareder and scareder. An' they called out, "Who's that a-knockin' at the door? Who? Who?"

An' the voice didn't say nothin', but the knockin' just kept on.

An' the dough kept a-swellin' an' a-swellin', an' the old conjure wives begun to scrooge up smaller an' smaller, an' their eyes got bigger an' bigger with scaredness, an' they kept a-callin', "Who's that a-knockin'? Who? Who?"

An' then the knockin' stopped, and the voice called out,

> *Fly out the window, do!*
> *There's no more house for you!*

An' the old conjure wives they spread their wings an' they flew out the windows an' off into the woods, all a-callin', "Who'll cook for you? Who? Who?"

An' now if you go into the woods in the dark o' the moon you'll see the old conjure wife owls an' hear 'em callin', "Who'll cook for you? Who-o! Who-o!"

Only on a Halloween night you don't want to go round the old owls, because *then* they turns to old conjure wives a-weavin' their spells.

FRANCES G. WICKES

Murdoch's Rath

There was not a nicer boy in all Ireland than Pat, and clever at his trade, too, if only he'd had one.

But from his cradle he learned nothing (small blame to him, with no one to teach him), so when he came to years of discretion he earned his living by running messages for his neighbors; and Pat could always be trusted to make the best of a bad bargain and bring back all the change, for he was the soul of honesty and good nature.

It's no wonder then that he was beloved by everyone and got as much work as he could do; and if the pay had but fitted the work, he'd have been mighty comfortable; but as it was, what he got wouldn't have kept him in shoe leather, but for making both ends meet by wearing his shoes in his pocket, except when he was in town and obliged to look genteel for the credit of the place he came from.

Well, all was going on as peaceable as could be, till one market-day, when business (or it might have been pleasure) detained him till the heel of the evening, and by nightfall, when he began to make the road short in good earnest, he was so flustered rehearsing his messages to make sure he'd forgotten nothing, that he never bethought him to leave off his brogues, but tramped on just as if shoe leather was made to be knocked to bits on the king's highway.

And this is what he was after saying:

"A dozen hanks of gray yarn for Mistress Murphy.

"Three gross of bright buttons for the tailor.

"Half an ounce of throat-drops for Father Andrew, and an ounce of snuff for his housekeeper," and so on.

For these were what he went to the town to fetch, and he was afraid lest one of the lot might have slipped his memory.

Now everybody knows there are two ways home from the town; and that's not meaning the right way and the wrong way, which my grandmother (rest her soul!) said there was to every place but one that it's not genteel to name. (There could only be a wrong way there, she said.) The two ways home from the town were the highway and the way by Murdoch's Rath.

Murdoch's Rath was a pleasant enough spot in the daytime, but not many persons cared to go by it when the sun was down. And in all the years Pat was going backwards and forwards, he never once came home except by the highroad till this unlucky evening, when, just at the place where the two roads part, he got, as one may say, into a sort of confusion.

"Halt!" says he to himself (for his own uncle had been a soldier, and Pat knew the word of command). "The left-hand turn is the right one," says he, and he was going down the high-road as straight as he could go, when suddenly he bethought himself. "And what am I doing?" he says. "This was my left hand going to town, and how in the name of fortune could it be my left going back, considering that I've turned round? It's well that I looked into it in time."

And with that he went off as fast down the other road as he had started down this. But how far he walked he never could tell, before all of a sudden the moon shone out as bright as day, and Pat found himself in Murdoch's Rath.

And this was the smallest part of the wonder; for the Rath was full of fairies.

When Pat got in, they were dancing round and round till his feet tingled to look at them, being a good dancer himself. And as he sat on the side of the Rath, and snapped his fingers to mark the time, the dancing stopped, and a little man comes up in a black hat and a green coat, with white stockings and red shoes on his feet.

"Won't you take a turn with us, Pat?" says he, bowing till he nearly touched the ground. And, indeed, he had not far to go, for he was barely two feet high.

"Don't say it twice, sir," says Pat. "It's myself will be proud to foot the floor wid ye"; and before you could look round, there was Pat in the circle dancing away for dear life.

At first his feet felt like feathers for lightness, and it seemed as if he could have gone on forever. But at last he grew tired, and would have liked to stop but the fairies would not, and so they danced on and on. Pat tried to think of something good to say, that he might free himself from the spell, but all he could think of was:

"A dozen hanks of gray yarn for Mistress Murphy."

"Three gross of bright buttons for the tailor."

"Half an ounce of throat-drops for Father Andrew, and an ounce of snuff for his housekeeper," and so on.

And it seemed to Pat that the moon was on the one side of the Rath when they began to dance, and on the other side when they left off; but he could not be sure after all that going round. One thing was plain enough. He danced every bit of leather off the soles of his feet, and they were blistered so that he could hardly stand; but all the little folk did was to stand and hold their sides with laughing at him.

At last the one who spoke before stepped up to him, and— "Don't break your heart about it, Pat," says he; "I'll lend you my own shoes till the morning, for you seem to be a good-natured sort of a boy."

Well, Pat looked at the fairy man's shoes that were the size of a baby's, and he looked at his own feet. But not wishing to be uncivil, "Thank ye kindly, sir," says he, "and if your honor'll be good enough to put them on for me, maybe you won't spoil the shape." For he thought to himself, "Small blame to me if the little gentleman can't get them to fit."

With that he sat down on the side of the Rath, and the fairy man put on the shoes for him, and no sooner did they touch Pat's feet than they became altogether a convenient size, and fitted him like wax. And, more than that, when he stood up, he didn't feel his blisters at all.

"Bring 'em back to the Rath at sunrise, Pat, my boy," says the little man.

And as Pat was climbing over the ditch, "Look round, Pat,"

says he. And when Pat looked round, there were jewels and pearls lying at the roots of the furze-bushes on the ditch, as thick as peas.

"Will you help yourself, or take what's given ye, Pat?" says the fairy man.

"Did I ever learn manners?" says Pat. "Would you have me help myself before company? I'll take what your honor pleases to give me, and be thankful."

The fairy man picked a lot of yellow furze-blossoms from the bushes, and filled Pat's pockets.

"Keep 'em for love, Pat, me darlin'," says he.

Pat would have liked some of the jewels, but he put the furze-blossoms by for love.

"Good evening to your honor," says he.

"And where are you going, Pat dear?" says the fairy man.

"I'm going home," says Pat. And if the fairy man didn't know where that was, small blame to him.

"Just let me dust those shoes for ye, Pat," says the fairy man. And as Pat lifted up each foot he breathed on it, and dusted it with the tail of his green coat.

"Home!" says he, and when he let go, Pat was at his own doorstep before he could look round, and his parcels safe and sound with him.

Next morning he was up with the sun, and carried the fairy man's shoes back to the Rath. As he came up, the little man looked over the ditch.

"The top of the morning to your honor," says Pat; "here's your shoes."

"You're an honest boy, Pat," says the little gentleman. "It's inconvenienced I am without them, for I have but the one pair. Have you looked at the yellow flowers this morning?" he says.

"I have not, sir," says Pat; "I'd be loath to deceive you. I came off as soon as I was up."

"Be sure to look when you get back, Pat," says the fairy man, "and good luck to ye!"

With which he disappeared, and Pat went home. He looked for the furze-blossoms, as the fairy man told him, and there's not a word of truth in this tale if they weren't all pure gold pieces.

Well, now Pat was so rich, he went to the shoemaker to order another pair of brogues, and being a kindly, gossiping boy, he soon told the shoemaker the whole story of the fairy man and the Rath. And this so stirred up the shoemaker's greed that he resolved to go the next night himself, to see if he could not dance with the fairies, and have like luck.

He found his way to the Rath all correct, and sure enough the fairies were dancing, and they asked him to join. He danced the soles off his brogues, as Pat did, and the fairy man lent him his shoes, and sent him home in a twinkling.

As he was going over the ditch, he looked round, and saw the roots of the furze-bushes glowing with precious stones as if they had been glow-worms.

"Will you help yourself, or take what's given ye?" said the fairy man.

"I'll help myself, if you please," said the cobbler, for he thought, "If I can't get more than Pat brought home, my fingers must all be thumbs."

So he drove his hand into the bushes, and if he didn't get plenty, it wasn't for want of grasping.

When he got up in the morning, he went straight to the jewels. But not a stone of the lot was more precious than roadside pebbles. "I ought not to look till I come from the Rath," said he. "It's best to do like Pat all through."

But he made up his mind not to return the fairy man's shoes.

"Who knows the virtue that's in them?" he said. So he made a small pair of red leather shoes, as like them as could be, and he blacked the others upon his feet, that the fairies might not know them, and at sunrise he went to the Rath.

The fairy man was looking over the ditch as before.

"Good morning to you," said he.

"The top of the morning to you, sir," said the cobbler; "here's your shoes." And he handed him the pair that he had made, with a face as grave as a judge.

The fairy man looked at them, but he said nothing, though he did not put them on.

"Have you looked at the things you got last night?" says he.

"I'll not deceive you, sir," said the cobbler. "I came off as soon as I was up. Sorra peep I took at them."

"Be sure to look when you get back," says the fairy man. And just as the cobbler was getting over the ditch to go home, he says, "If my eyes don't deceive me," says he, "there's the least taste in life of dirt on your left shoe. Let me dust it with the tail of my coat."

"That means home in a twinkling," thought the cobbler, and he held up his foot.

The fairy man dusted it, and muttered something the cobbler did not hear. Then, "Sure," says he, "it's the dirty pastures that you've come through, for the other shoe's as bad."

So the cobbler held up his right foot, and the fairy man rubbed that with the tail of his green coat.

When all was done, the cobbler's feet seemed to tingle, and then to itch, and then to smart, and then to burn. And at last he began to dance, and he danced all round the Rath (the fairy man laughing and holding his sides) and then round and round again. And he danced till he cried out with weariness and tried to shake the shoes off. But they stuck fast, and the fairies drove him over the ditch, and through the prickly furze-bushes, and he danced away. Where he danced to, I cannot tell you. Whether he ever got rid of the fairy shoes I do not know. The jewels never were more than wayside pebbles, and they were swept out when his cabin was cleaned, which was not too soon, you may be sure.

All this happened long ago; but there are those who say that the covetous cobbler dances still, between sunset and sunrise, round Murdoch's Rath.

JULIANA H. EWING

The Strange Visitor

A woman was sitting at her reel one night;
And still she sat, and still she reeled, and
   still she wished for company.

In came a pair of broad broad soles, and sat
   down at the fireside;
And still she sat, and still she reeled, and
   still she wished for company.

In came a pair of small small legs, and sat
   down on the broad broad soles;
And still she sat, and still she reeled, and
   still she wished for company.

In came a pair of thick thick knees, and sat down
   on the small small legs;
And still she sat, and still she reeled, and still
   she wished for company.

In came a pair of thin thin thighs, and sat down
   on the thick thick knees;
And still she sat, and still she reeled, and still
   she wished for company.

In came a pair of huge huge hips, and sat down
   on the thin thin thighs;
And still she sat, and still she reeled, and still
   she wished for company.

In came a wee wee waist, and sat down
   on the huge huge hips;
And still she sat, and still she reeled, and still
   she wished for company.

In came a pair of broad broad shoulders, and sat
   down on the wee wee waist;
And still she sat, and still she reeled, and still
   she wished for company.

In came a pair of small small arms, and sat down
   on the broad broad shoulders;
And still she sat, and still she reeled, and still
   she wished for company.

In came a pair of huge huge hands, and sat down
   on the small small arms;
And still she sat, and still she reeled, and still
   she wished for company.

In came a small small neck, and sat down on the
    broad broad shoulders;
And still she sat, and still she reeled, and still
    she wished for company.

In came a huge huge head, and sat down on the
    small small neck.

"How did you get such broad broad feet?" quoth
    the woman.
"Much tramping, much tramping" (*gruffly*).

"How did you get such small small legs?"
"*Aih-h-h!*—late—and *wee-e-e*—moul" (*whiningly*).

"How did you get such thick thick knees?"
"Much praying, much praying" (*piously*).

"How did you get such thin thin thighs?"
"Aih-h-h!—late—and wee-e-e—moul" (*whiningly*).

"How did you get such big big hips?"
"Much sitting, much sitting" (*gruffly*).

"How did you get such a wee wee waist?"
"Aih-h-h!—late—and wee-e-e—moul" (*whiningly*).

"How did you get such broad broad shoulders?"
"With carrying broom, with carrying broom" (*gruffly*).

"How did you get such small small arms?"
"Aih-h-h!—late—and wee-e-e—moul" (*whiningly*).

"How did you get such huge huge hands?"
"Threshing with an iron flail, threshing with an
    iron flail" (*gruffly*).

"How did you get such a small small neck?"
"Aih-h-h!—late—and wee-e-e—moul" (*pitifully*).

"How did you get such a huge huge head?"
"Much knowledge, much knowledge" (*keenly*).

"What do you come for?"
"FOR YOU!" (*At the top of the voice, with a wave
   of the arm, and a stamp of the feet.*)

JOSEPH JACOBS

⤙ *Part Five*
PRINCES, PRINCESSES, EMPERORS AND KINGS

The Magic Fishbone

There was once a king, and he had a queen; and he was the manliest of his sex, and she was the loveliest of hers. The king was, in his private profession, under government. The queen's father had been a medical man out of town.

They had nineteen children, and were always having more. Seventeen of these children took care of the baby; and Alicia, the eldest, took care of them all. Their ages varied from seven to seven months.

Let us now resume our story.

One day the king was going to the office, when he stopped at the fishmonger's to buy a pound and a half of salmon not too near the tail, which the queen (who was a careful housekeeper) had requested him to send home. Mr. Pickles, the fishmonger, said, "Certainly, sir; is there any other article? Good morning."

The king went on towards the office in a melancholy mood; for quarter-day was such a long way off, and several of the dear children were growing out of their clothes. He had not proceeded far when Mr. Pickles's errand-boy came running after him and said, "Sir, you didn't notice the old lady in our shop."

"What old lady?" inquired the king. "I saw none."

Now, the king had not seen any old lady, because this old lady had been invisible to him, though visible to Mr. Pickles's boy. Probably because he messed and splashed the water about to that degree, and flopped the pairs of soles down in that violent manner, that, if she had not been visible to him, he would have spoilt her clothes.

Just then the old lady came trotting up. She was dressed in shot-silk of the richest quality, smelling of dried lavender.

194

"King Watkins the First, I believe?" said the old lady.

"Watkins," replied the king, "is my name."

"Papa, if I am not mistaken, of the beautiful Princess Alicia?" said the old lady.

"And of eighteen other darlings," replied the king.

"Listen. You are going to the office," said the old lady.

It instantly flashed upon the king that she must be a fairy, or how could she know that?

"You are right," said the old lady, answering his thoughts. "I am the good Fairy Grandmarina. Attend! When you return home to dinner, politely invite the Princess Alicia to have some of the salmon you bought just now."

"It may disagree with her," said the king. The old lady became so very angry at this absurd idea that the king was quite alarmed and humbly begged her pardon.

"We hear a great deal too much about this thing disagreeing and that thing disagreeing," said the old lady with the greatest contempt it was possible to express. "Don't be greedy. I think you want it all yourself."

The king hung his head under this reproof and said he wouldn't talk about things disagreeing any more.

"Be good, then," said the Fairy Grandmarina, "and don't! When the beautiful Princess Alicia consents to partake of the salmon—as I think she will—you will find she will leave a fish-bone on her plate. Tell her to dry it, and to rub it, and to polish it till it shines like mother-of-pearl, and to take care of it as a present from me."

"Is that all?" asked the king.

"Don't be impatient, sir," returned the Fairy Grandmarina, scolding him severely. "Don't catch people short before they have done speaking. Just the way with you grown-up persons. You are always doing it."

The king again hung his head and said he wouldn't do so any more.

"Be good, then," said the Fairy Grandmarina, "and don't! Tell the Princess Alicia, with my love, that the fishbone is a magic present which can only be used once; but that it will bring her, that once, whatever she wishes for, *provided she wishes for it at the right time*. That is the message. Take care of it."

The king was beginning, "Might I ask the reason?" when the fairy became absolutely furious.

"*Will* you be good, sir?" she exclaimed, stamping her foot on the ground. "The reason for this, and the reason for that, indeed! You are always wanting the reason. No reason. There! Hoity toity me! I am sick of your grown-up reasons."

The king was extremely frightened by the old lady's flying into such a passion, and he said he was very sorry to have offended her, and he wouldn't ask for reasons any more.

"Be good, then," said the old lady, "and don't!"

With those words, Grandmarina vanished, and the king went on and on and on till he came to the office. There he wrote and wrote and wrote till it was time to go home again. Then he politely invited the Princess Alicia, as the fairy had directed him, to partake of the salmon. And when she had enjoyed it very much, he saw the fishbone on her plate, as the fairy had told him he would, and he delivered the fairy's message, and the Princess Alicia took care to *dry* the bone, and to *rub* it, and to *polish* it, till it shone like mother-of-pearl.

And so, when the queen was going to get up in the morning, she said, "Oh, dear me, dear me; my head, my head!" and then she fainted away.

The Princess Alicia, who happened to be looking in at the chamber door, asking about breakfast, was very much alarmed when she saw her royal mamma in this state, and she rang the bell for Peggy, which was the name of the lord chamberlain. But remembering where the smelling-bottle was, she climbed on a chair and got it; and after that she climbed on another chair to the bedside, and held the smelling-bottle to the queen's nose; and after that she jumped down and got some water; and after that she jumped up again and wetted the queen's forehead; and, in short, when the lord chamberlain came in, that dear old woman said to the little princess, "What a trot you are! I couldn't have done it better myself!"

But that was not the worst of the good queen's illness. Oh, no! She was very ill indeed, for a long time.

The Princess Alicia kept the seventeen young princes and princesses quiet, and dressed and undressed and danced the baby, and made the kettle boil, and heated the soup, and swept the hearth, and poured out the medicine, and nursed the queen, and did all that ever she could, and was as busy, busy, busy, as busy as could be; for there were not many servants at that palace for three reasons: because the king was short of money, because a rise in his office never seemed to come, and because quarter-day was so far off that it looked almost as far off and as little as one of the stars.

But on the morning when the queen fainted away, where was the magic fishbone? Why, there it was in the Princess Alicia's pocket! She had almost taken it out to bring the queen to life again when she put it back and looked for the smelling-bottle.

After the queen had come out of her swoon that morning and was dozing, the Princess Alicia hurried upstairs to tell a most particular secret to a most particular confidential friend of hers, who was a duchess. People did suppose her to be a doll; but she was really a duchess, though nobody knew it except the princess.

This most particular secret was the secret about the magic fish-bone, the history of which was well known to the duchess because the princess told her everything. The princess kneeled down by the bed on which the duchess was lying, full-dressed and wide-awake, and whispered the secret to her. The duchess smiled and nodded. People might have supposed that she never smiled and nodded; but she often did, though nobody knew it except the princess.

Then the Princess Alicia hurried downstairs again to keep watch in the queen's room. She often kept watch by herself in the queen's room; but every evening, while the illness lasted, she sat there watching with the king. And every evening the king sat looking at her with a cross look, wondering why she never brought out the magic fishbone.

As often as she noticed this, she ran upstairs, whispered the secret to the duchess over again, and said to the duchess besides, "They think we children never have a reason or a meaning!" And the duchess, though the most fashionable duchess that ever was heard of, winked her eye.

"Alicia," said the king, one evening, when she wished him good night.

"Yes, Papa."

"What has become of the magic fishbone?"

"In my pocket, Papa!"

"I thought you had lost it!"

"Oh, no, Papa!"

"Or forgotten it?"

"No, indeed, Papa."

And so another time the little snapping pug dog next door made a rush at one of the young princes as he stood on the steps coming home from school, and frightened him out of his wits; and he put his hand through a pane of glass and bled, bled, bled. When the seventeen other young princes and princesses saw him bleed, bleed, bleed, they were frightened out of their wits too, and screamed themselves black in their seventeen faces all at once.

But the Princess Alicia put her hands over all their seventeen mouths, one after another, and persuaded them to be quiet because of the sick queen. And then she put the wounded prince's hand in a basin of fresh cold water, while they stared with their twice seventeen are thirty-four, put down four and carry three, eyes, and then she looked in the hand for bits of glass, and there were fortunately no bits of glass there. And then she said to two chubby-legged princes, who were sturdy though small, "Bring me in the royal rag-bag: I must snip and stitch and cut and contrive." So the two young princes tugged at the royal rag-bag and lugged it in; and the Princess Alicia sat down on the floor, with a large pair of scissors and a needle and thread, and snipped and stitched and cut and contrived, and made a bandage, and put it on, and it fitted beautifully; and so when it was all done, she saw the king her papa looking on by the door.

"Alicia."

"Yes, Papa."

"What have you been doing?"

"Snipping, stitching, cutting, and contriving, Papa."

"Where is the magic fishbone?"

"In my pocket, Papa."

"I thought you had lost it."

"Oh, no, Papa!"

"Or forgotten it?"

"No, indeed, Papa."

After that, she ran upstairs to the duchess, and told her what had passed, and told her the secret over again; and the duchess shook her flaxen curls, and laughed with her rosy lips.

Well! and so another time the baby fell under the grate. The seventeen young princes and princesses were used to it, for they were almost always falling under the grate or down the stairs; but the baby was not used to it yet, and it gave him a swelled face and a black eye.

The way the poor little darling came to tumble was, that he was out of the Princess Alicia's lap just as she was sitting, in a great coarse apron that quite smothered her, in front of the

kitchen fire, beginning to peel the turnips for the broth for dinner; and the way she came to be doing that was that the king's
cook had run away that morning with her own true love, who was
a very tall but very tipsy soldier.

Then the seventeen young princes and princesses, who cried at
everything that happened, cried and roared. But the Princess
Alicia (who couldn't help crying a little herself) quietly called to
them to be still, on account of not throwing back the queen upstairs, who was fast getting well, and said, "Hold your tongues,
you wicked little monkeys, every one of you, while I examine
Baby!"

Then she examined Baby and found that he hadn't broken
anything; and she held cold iron to his poor dear eye, and
smoothed his poor dear face, and he presently fell asleep in her
arms. Then she said to the seventeen princes and princesses, "I
am afraid to let him down yet, lest he should wake and feel pain;
be good, and you shall all be cooks."

They jumped for joy when they heard that, and began making
themselves cooks' caps out of old newspapers. So to one she gave
the salt-box, and to one she gave the barley, and to one she gave
the herbs, and to one she gave the turnips, and to one she gave the
carrots, and to one she gave the onions, and to one she gave the
spice-box, till they were all cooks, and all running about at work,
she sitting in the middle, smothered in the great coarse apron,
nursing Baby.

By and by the broth was done; and the baby woke up, smiling
like an angel, and was trusted to the sedatest princess to hold,
while the other princes and princesses were squeezed into a far-
off corner to look at the Princess Alicia turning out the saucepan-
ful of broth, for fear (as they were always getting into trouble)
they should get splashed and scalded. When the broth came
tumbling out, steaming beautifully, and smelling like a nosegay
good to eat, they clapped their hands. That made the baby clap
his hands; and that, and his looking as if he had a comic tooth-
ache, made all the princes and princesses laugh. So the Princess
Alicia said, "Laugh and be good; and after dinner we will make
him a nest on the floor in a corner, and he shall sit in his nest and
see a dance of eighteen cooks."

That delighted the young princes and princesses, and they ate up all the broth, and washed up all the plates and dishes, and cleared away, and pushed the table into a corner; and then they in their cooks' caps, and the Princess Alicia in the smothering coarse apron that belonged to the cook that had run away with her own true love that was the very tall but very tipsy soldier, danced a dance of eighteen cooks before the angelic baby, who forgot his swelled face and his black eye and crowed with joy.

And so then, once more, the Princess Alicia saw King Watkins the First, her father, standing in the doorway looking on, and he said, "What have you been doing, Alicia?"

"Cooking and contriving, Papa."

"What else have you been doing, Alicia?"

"Keeping the children lighthearted, Papa."

"Where is the magic fishbone, Alicia?"

"In my pocket, Papa."

"I thought you had lost it?"

"Oh, no, Papa!"

"Or forgotten it?"

"No, indeed, Papa."

The king then sighed so heavily, and seemed so low-spirited, and sat down so miserably, leaning his head upon his hand, and his elbow upon the kitchen table pushed away in the corner, that the seventeen princes and princesses crept softly out of the kitchen and left him alone with the Princess Alicia and the angelic baby.

"What is the matter, Papa?"

"I am dreadfully poor, my child."

"Have you no money at all, Papa?"

"None, my child."

"Is there no way of getting any, Papa?"

"No way," said the king. "I have tried very hard, and I have tried all ways." When she heard those last words, the Princess Alicia began to put her hand into the pocket where she kept the magic fishbone.

"Papa," said she. "When we have tried very hard, and tried all ways, we must have done our very, very best?"

"No doubt, Alicia."

"When we have done our very, very best, Papa, and that is not enough, then I think the right time must have come for asking help of others." This was the very secret connected with the magic fishbone, which she had found out for herself from the good Fairy Grandmarina's words, and which she had so often whispered to her beautiful and fashionable friend the duchess.

So she took out of her pocket the magic fishbone that had been dried and rubbed and polished till it shone like mother-of-pearl; and she gave it one little kiss, and wished it was quarter-day. And immediately it *was* quarter-day; and the king's quarter's salary came rattling down the chimney and bounced into the middle of the floor.

But this was not half of what happened—no, not a quarter; for immediately afterwards the good Fairy Grandmarina came riding in, in a carriage and four (peacocks), with Mr. Pickles's boy up behind, dressed in silver and gold, with a cocked hat, powdered hair, pink silk stockings, a jeweled cane, and a nose-gay. Down jumped Mr. Pickles's boy, with his cocked hat in his hand, and wonderfully polite (being entirely changed by enchantment), and handed Grandmarina out; and there she stood, in her rich shot-silk smelling of dried lavender, fanning herself with a sparkling fan.

"Alicia, my dear," said this charming old fairy, "how do you do? I hope I see you pretty well? Give me a kiss."

The Princess Alicia embraced her; and then Grandmarina turned to the king and said rather sharply, "Are you good?"

The king said he hoped so.

"I suppose you know the reason *now* why my goddaughter here," kissing the princess again, "did not apply to the fishbone sooner?" said the fairy.

The king made a shy bow.

"Ah! but you didn't *then?*" said the fairy.

The king made a shyer bow.

"Any more questions to ask?" said the fairy. The king said no, and he was very sorry.

"Be good, then," said the fairy, "and live happy ever afterwards."

Then Grandmarina waved her fan, and the queen came in most splendidly dressed; and the seventeen young princes and princesses, no longer grown out of their clothes, came in, newly fitted out from top to toe, with tucks in everything to admit of its being let out. After that, the fairy tapped the Princess Alicia with her fan; and the smothering coarse apron flew away, and she appeared exquisitely dressed, like a little bride, with a wreath of orange blossoms and a silver veil. After that, the kitchen dresser changed of itself into a wardrobe made of beautiful woods and gold and looking-glass, which was full of dresses of all sorts, all for her and all exactly fitting her. After that, the angelic baby came in running alone, with his face and eye not a bit the worse, but much the better. Then Grandmarina begged to be introduced to the duchess; and, when the duchess was brought down, many compliments passed between them.

A little whispering took place between the fairy and the duchess; and then the fairy said out loud, "Yes, I thought she would have told you." Grandmarina then turned to the king and queen, and said, "We are going in search of Prince Certainpersonio. The pleasure of your company is requested at church in half an hour precisely." So she and the Princess Alicia got into the carriage; and Mr. Pickles's boy handed in the duchess, who sat by herself on the opposite seat; and then Mr. Pickles's boy put up the steps and got up behind, and the peacocks flew away with their tails behind.

Prince Certainpersonio was sitting by himself, eating barley-sugar, and waiting to be ninety. When he saw the peacocks, followed by the carriage, coming in at the window, it immediately occurred to him that something uncommon was going to happen.

"Prince," said Grandmarina, "I bring you your bride."

The moment the fairy said those words, Prince Certainpersonio's face left off being sticky, and his jacket and corduroys changed to peach-bloom velvet, and his hair curled, and a cap and feather flew in like a bird and settled on his head. He got into the carriage by the fairy's invitation; and there he renewed his acquaintance with the duchess, whom he had seen before.

In the church were the prince's relations and friends, and the

Princess Alicia's relations and friends, and the seventeen princes and princesses, and the baby, and a crowd of the neighbors. The marriage was beautiful beyond expression. The duchess was bridesmaid and beheld the ceremony from the pulpit, where she was supported by the cushion of the desk.

Grandmarina gave a magnificent wedding feast afterwards, in which there was everything and more to eat, and everything and more to drink. The wedding cake was delicately ornamented with white satin ribbons, frosted silver, and white lilies, and was forty-two yards round.

When Grandmarina had drunk her love to the young couple, and Prince Certainpersonio had made a speech, and everybody had cried, "Hip, hip, hip, hurrah!" Grandmarina announced to the king and queen that in the future there would be eight quarter-days in every year, except in leap year, when there would be ten. She then turned to Certainpersonio and Alicia and said, "My dears, you will have thirty-five children, and they will all be good and beautiful. Seventeen of your children will be boys, and eighteen will be girls. The hair of the whole of your children will curl naturally. They will never have the measles, and will have recovered from the whooping-cough before being born."

On hearing such good news, everybody cried out, "Hip, hip, hip, hurrah!" again.

"It only remains," said Grandmarina in conclusion, "to make an end of the fishbone."

So she took it from the hand of the Princess Alicia, and it instantly flew down the throat of the little snapping pug-dog next door.

CHARLES DICKENS

Companions of the Forest

A long time ago there lived in Calabria, in the south of Italy, a poor boy called Caesarino di Berni. A promising lad he was, clever, handsome, good-humored, and a kind and helpful son to his widowed mother. He had no boy companions of his own age, but he did not miss them, and I will tell you why.

One day he had wandered far into a neighboring forest, and there in the thickest part he came upon a huge cavern. On examining it he found it was divided into three caves. In one of these he found a litter of bear-cubs; in another, a litter of wolf-cubs; in the third were little lions cuddled together. Their mothers had left them when they were just of an age to begin to fend for themselves; but they were still the prettiest, playfullest things you can imagine. Caesarino took one of each home with him and fed them, and in time they became his favorite pets. In their turn they grew very fond of him and of each other; nor were they ever anything but gentle with the other folk about the house. When they grew bigger, Caesarino trained them to hunt. Early in the morning, before anyone was about, he would be up and off with them to the forest, where they spent long, happy days together.

If he taught them hunting, according to a method of his own, they taught him all kinds of forest lore, of which wild animals know more than men. When night came on and he brought them back, he was laden with spoil. By this means, as the years went on, he grew rich and was able to support his mother and sisters in great comfort. Of course, the few neighbors they had wondered very much about the source of their prosperity; but as they were not hunters, and never went into the forest, they did not find out for themselves. Now Caesarino, though helpful to his neighbors,

warned his family not to tell how he spent his days, lest some jealous person should harm his faithful helpers or steal them away.

But his sisters forgot their promise, and chattered about their brother's hunting to the folks around; and one day a neighbor said to him, "You are a sulky kind of fellow, surely! Good friends as we are, you never take me with you when you go out. I hear you have become a mighty hunter. Now nothing would please me better than to spend a day in the forest with you."

Caesarino answered neither yea nor nay; but to himself he said, "My secret is out. It is time I left this place, lest evil should befall my three good friends."

So, leaving all his possessions to his mother and sisters, he set out into the world to seek his fortune. Of course, the wolf, the bear and the lion went with him; and the four were the best of company to each other on the road. At last they reached the seashore. There they went on board a ship and landed in Sicily. After long travel over hill and dale, they came one day to a beautiful and very lonely place where stood a hermitage. The sun was blazing hot over their heads; and they entered for rest and shelter. Shortly after, the hermit came home. At the sight of the wild animals in his hut he started and called out for terror; but Caesarino said, "Fear nothing, good father. They will not harm you." No one looked on Caesarino without trusting him; so the hermit was satisfied, and, poor man though he was, he found bread and wine to give to his guest, who was hungry and tired. The three beasts foraged for themselves, and all the five supped merrily together.

"A fine country this!" said Caesarino to the old man.

"You think so?" was his reply. "Ah, you do not know. Ours is indeed a most unhappy country! Near this place there hides a horrid, fearsome dragon. When he comes out of his lair his poisonous breath destroys all that come near him. You see how solitary it is. That is because all our people are leaving the land. Moreover, the monster demands that every day a human creature shall be offered him for his food. Were this refused, he would come out and devour the inhabitants far and near. Many poor folks have been thrown to him to stay his appetite; but he only gets greedier and greedier, and daintier and daintier; and now— what do you think?—he demands for his dinner tomorrow no one less than the beautiful young Princess Dorothea, the daughter of our King!"

"And no man goes forth to slay this horrid creature?" asked Caesarino, with spirit.

"It is impossible! No man dares! The poor King is wild with grief, but for the sake of his people he must give her up."

"I think the maiden will not die just yet," said Caesarino, quietly.

Next morning he was up and away betimes with his three companions before the hermit was awake. The four betook themselves to the place ordained for the sacrifice, where the king's daughter was already placed. Alone she stood in the middle of the road, her cowardly attendants having all fled. He looked on her beauty for a brief instant and his heart was filled with pity, but she seemed turned to stone with terror, and neither saw nor heard his approach. And, indeed, as he looked, on rushed the horrid monster towards her, his jaws open, his fiery eyes gleaming with savage delight at the thought of the delicate morsel awaiting him. Much too eager and ravenous was he to take any heed of the young man standing by. And if he had, what could a mere stripling do?

But Caesarino, just at the right moment, spurred on his animals, and with splendid courage they rushed to the attack, gripping the creature from behind and avoiding his poisonous breath. The dragon struggled fiercely; but he was powerless in their

grip; and after a desperate combat, which lasted for some minutes, he fell on the road quite dead.

Caesarino called to the fainting damsel to arise and have no fear, and bade her run to her attendants, who stood trembling at a distance, and go home at once with them to her father. Then with his wood-knife he cut out the dragon's tongue, put it in his wallet, and went away with his three friends as quietly as if he encountered a dragon every morning of his life. All he said to the hermit on entering the hut was, "You may now sleep in peace. The country is safe. The dragon is no more."

But soon after Caesarino had left the place of the sacrifice, a certain man passed the spot, and spied the dead monster. A rude, clownish, ruffianly person he was!

"Aha!" said he, "the King promised the Princess in marriage to whoever should slay the dragon. I'll have her!" So saying, he took out a cutlass he wore in his belt, and struck off the creature's head, put it in a sack, and raced off to the city and the king's palace with it as hard as ever he could. As he entered the gates the bells were ringing peals of joy; the people were in the streets singing, or cheering in front of the palace. The ruffian—Grechio was his name—made his way easily enough into the royal presence, for all doors were open at such a time; and falling on his knees before the king, he said, "It was I, sire, who killed the dragon! Now I claim the reward—your daughter as my wife!"

"You killed the dragon! You? But I must have some proof of it," said the king.

"See my proof," returned Grechio.

He took out the dragon's head and held it up before them all; and the assembled people in their joy cried, "Long live Grechio! Grechio shall wed her!"

Now as for Dorothea, she had been in too fainting a condition during the combat with the monster to know what her deliverer looked like. But her heart sank at the thought of so churlish a husband as the one standing before her. And the king said to himself, "Must I really have this boor for my son-in-law?" Nevertheless, a king's word is sacred; and he ordered that great feasting should be held in his capital and throughout his kingdom. He himself was to give a splendid banquet in honor of the event.

Now the hermit, who used to come into the city every day to beg his bread, heard of all the feasting that had been ordered; and he was told the story of the great champion Grechio. "Did that goodly youth, my guest, then lie to me?" he said. So he went back to his hermitage and told Caesarino all that folks were saying in the town.

Caesarino laughed and said, "Ah, he cut off the head, did he? I can show something more convincing than that." And he took the tongue from his wallet and held it up. "See here! Is this not enough?"

"Come with me at once to the King," said the hermit. So he and Caesarino and the lion, the bear, and the wolf set off for the city and the king's palace. While the old man made his way into the presence-chamber, the others waited at the door. Kneeling before the king, the hermit said, "I have heard with great concern that your Majesty is about to give your fair daughter, Dorothea, in marriage to a rough clown, who will be no good king for your people when it shall please God to call you hence. But the fellow is not only a clown; he is a liar as well; and with your permission I will bring the real champion before you."

"My good man," said the king, "a promise is a promise. And whatever I may think of Prince Grechio"—they called him Prince by this time—"he has brought me clear proof that he it was rid my kingdom of that terrible scourge."

"Then," replied the hermit, "I beg, sire, that you will order the head of the monster to be brought here." And the horrid thing was brought, and held up in the sight of all.

"Open its jaws," said the hermit. And they opened its jaws. "But where is its tongue?" They looked: there was no tongue!

Then at a signal Caesarino and his companions came forward. The bystanders looked with wonder and admiration at the fine young man, so tall and fair and noble of bearing—though they drew back at the sight of his hairy friends.

"I bring what is missing, your Majesty," said the youth; and from his wallet he drew forth the great tongue. Then opening the jaws, he put it into the horrid mouth; and, lo, it fitted exactly!

By this time Grechio, who had been standing near, trembling the while, saw that his falsehood was discovered; and now he made a sudden movement toward the door. But the king cried, "Seize him, guards! Do not let him go!" And they seized him and flung him into prison, where he was given time for repentance.

After the guards had borne away the false pretender, the king ordered Caesarino to tell them how it came about that he, a stranger, was the champion of the princess and the deliverer of their land. He told his story modestly, adding, "But for all this I should have no praise. It was not I killed the dragon, but my three faithful friends here." And he dragged forward the three beasts and showed them to the king, who caressed them with smiles and tears of gratitude.

So Caesarino, not Grechio, was the bridegroom at the wedding the next week, and if the king rejoiced over so goodly a son-in-law, Dorothea rejoiced a great deal more.

As for the lion, the bear, and the wolf, neither the king nor the princess, nor the lords and ladies of the court could make enough of them. And when Caesarino at last reigned in the old king's stead, they were still his happy and trusty companions, just as they had been when as a poor lad he had hunted with them for his living in his native forests, and when he had set out in their company to seek his fortune.

> *And thus, and thus the story ran.*
> *Tell me a better if you can.*

ANNE MACDONNELL

Benito the Faithful

Once in the first times there was a poor boy named Benito who lived in a small village with his father and mother. He was very devoted to them. Benito often thought of leaving the village so that he could seek his fortune and help his parents in their struggle to earn a living. But he did not know how to do this.

However, after wishing for years that some opportunity would present itself, he had an idea. He was seated at the noonday meal with his father, who began to tell Benito of a young king who lived some distance from their village. He spoke of the beautiful palace in which the king lived, and of the number of servants that were employed there. It was then that Benito decided what he would do.

"That is the very thing for me!" he exclaimed. "I will go to the king and ask him to take me on as one of his servants, and I shall serve him well and make my fortune."

Benito's mother was reluctant to let her son leave home, but he pleaded so hard that at last both parents gave their consent.

And so it was the very next day, after his mother had prepared a lunch for him to carry, that Benito bade his parents good-bye and started on his journey. He walked and walked until at last he reached the king's palace. He had some trouble in obtaining permission to see the king, but Benito, though weary, was determined, and at last the courtiers relented and he was taken before the young ruler.

His Majesty was very much impressed by the boy's sincerity and charm of manner. When Benito explained that he wished to earn money to help his old parents, the king decided to employ

him as one of his personal servants. And Benito was very glad and willing to work hard and do as he was told.

One day not long after his arrival at the palace, Benito was called into the presence of the king.

"Benito," said the king—knowing well the difficulty of the task he was unwilling to undertake himself—"I am going to entrust you with an important mission. If you succeed, all well and good. But if you fail you shall be punished."

Then he explained that he wished Benito to make a long journey to a kingdom across the sea where he was to find a certain princess and bring her back to him.

"That I will do, my lord," Benito promised.

On that same day the lad made ready for his long journey and set out. After having traveled a long way, he found himself in the heart of a dense wood. While he was walking, he was surprised to notice a large bird flying close to him, and that the bird's flight was made difficult by many strings that were tangled in its wings. While he watched, the bird spoke to him.

"Ah, my friend, I know that you will help me! Please loosen these strings in which I have become entangled. If you will do

that, I promise you that I will come to your aid whenever you call upon me."

Benito soon released the bird. Then he asked its name. The bird replied "Sparrow-hawk!" and was gone.

When Benito had continued his journey farther he found himself by the side of the sea. What could he do now? He had no way of getting across. As he stood there sadly looking out upon the water and thinking that he had failed, a huge fish swam up to him.

"Why are you looking so sad, my son?" asked the fish.

"I must cross this sea to find the princess for my master," the lad replied. "But I do not know how to get across."

"I am the King of Fishes," said the great fish. "If you get upon my back I will take you to the other side."

As soon as Benito was safely on the other side of the sea, he thanked the King of Fishes and bade him good day, for he wanted to be on his way. While he was wondering where to turn next, a beautiful fairy appeared to him and offered to help him. She seemed to know why Benito had come.

"The princess you seek is locked up in a castle which is guarded by wicked giants," she informed him. "To set her free, Benito, you will have to fight the giants. Take this magic sword." And she handed him a sword. "It has great power and will kill instantly anything it touches."

Benito was very grateful for the magic sword. He felt that with it he could overcome the giants no matter how strong they were. So he hurried on to the castle.

Before he had come even close to the castle he could see the immense giants who guarded it. If it had not been for his sword he would have been frightened. As it was, he approached fearlessly. When the giants saw Benito coming toward them they were so certain they could overpower him that they failed to arm themselves. Several of them walked up to him with great, huge strides, but as each one approached, Benito touched him with his magic weapon, and one by one the giants fell dead. At this, the other giants who stood watching were filled with such fear they ran for their lives.

It was now an easy matter for Benito to free the princess. "I am taking you to my master, who wishes to marry you," Benito explained to her.

They had no trouble in crossing the ocean, because the King of the Fishes was waiting for them. Willingly, he took the two of them across the waters to the other side. Then, after journeying through the forest, they reached the palace and were received with much rejoicing.

The king wished to celebrate his marriage with the princess, but when he asked her to marry him, she replied, "Not until I have my ring back."

"Where is your ring?" asked his Majesty.

"My lord, I dropped it into the depths of the sea while Benito and I were traveling here."

When the king heard that, he called for Benito once more and commanded that he find the princess's ring and bring it to her.

Benito promised that he would, but as he journeyed back to the sea once again, his heart was troubled to know how he was to search for the ring.

But once more the King of Fishes came to him. "Why are you so sad, Benito?"

Benito replied, "Alas, the princess dropped her ring into the ocean as you were taking us upon your back. I have been sent to find it. But how am I to do that?"

The King of Fishes told Benito not to be troubled any longer. And then he called to him all the fishes of the sea. But when they had assembled, he noticed that one fish was not there. He ordered the others to search for the missing fish.

Not long afterward several of the larger fishes found the missing one lying under a stone at the bottom of the sea. They told him to go at once to their king, but the fish said, "I am too full to swim. I have eaten too much." So the others dragged him into the presence of the King of Fishes.

"Why did you not obey me and come when I called?" asked the King of Fishes.

"I have eaten so much that I could not swim, your Majesty."

And straightway the fish king suspected what had happened. He ordered the fish to be cut open. When this had been done, they found the princess's ring, which the greedy fish had swallowed.

Benito was overjoyed to find the missing ring. He took it and thanked the King of Fishes for his help. At the end of that day he was once more back at the palace where he gave the missing ring to his master.

Without thanking his faithful servant, the king took the ornament to the princess and said, "Now that you have your ring, will you become my wife?"

"Not until I have my earring returned to me," replied the princess.

"Where is your earring?" the monarch asked impatiently.

"I lost it in the forest through which Benito and I journeyed on our way to the palace."

Again Benito was summoned to the king, and although sorely in need of rest, he was commanded to find the lost earring immediately.

Poor Benito, so weary after his previous adventures, nevertheless started out at once. By morning he had reached the deep forest. All day he searched faithfully along the paths which he and the princess had traveled. But in vain. At last, too weary to go farther, he sat down under a tree to rest.

While he was resting and feeling discouraged, a distinguished-looking mouse walked up to him.

"Why are you so sad, Benito?" the mouse inquired.

"Alas, I am searching for an earring which the princess lost while she and I were traveling through this forest. But how am I to find it in this vast place?"

"Do not be troubled any longer," said the kindly animal. "I am the King of Mice and I will find the earring for you."

Then the King of Mice called all the mice of the forest to him. One mouse was missing. The mouse king commanded that the others find the absent one. So they all went to search and soon found the missing mouse lying down under some bamboo trees.

The others told him to go at once to the King of Mice. "I am too full to walk," he said.

So they pulled him along until at last he stood before the master mouse.

"Why did you not come when I summoned you?" the king mouse asked sternly.

"I was too full to walk, Your Majesty," the mouse replied.

Then, suspecting what had happened, the King of Mice ordered the mouse to be opened up, and sure enough they found within it the missing earring.

Benito was overjoyed to find the earring. Thanking the mouse king, he made haste to return to the palace, where he immediately gave the earring to his master.

When the king restored the missing earring to the princess, he asked eagerly, "Now will you become my wife?"

And the princess answered, "I have only one more thing to ask of you, O King. If you will grant it I shall become your wife."

"Whatever it is, it shall be granted," the king told her, resignedly.

"Then," the princess said, "if you will get me some water from heaven and some water from the nether world, my last wish will be granted and gladly I shall become your wife."

Once more the weary but faithful Benito was summoned and once more given his orders.

"Bring me some water from heaven and some water from the nether world!" the king commanded.

Benito promised that he would. Again he set out, traveling once more to the forest. But once there, he did not know which way to turn to fulfill his mission. While he was wondering what to do he recalled the promise made to him by the large bird he had aided. He called, "Sparrow-hawk! Sparrow-hawk!" And in no time at all the big bird appeared.

Benito explained to it what he was searching for, and the bird said, "Be troubled no longer, Benito. I will get the waters for you."

Then the sparrow-hawk told Benito to make two cups from bamboo, and fasten one to each of his legs. This Benito did. The bamboo cups were very light and did not hinder the bird's flight. Watching him fly away, Benito wondered if he would ever see the sparrow-hawk again. But before nightfall he was back. Each of the cups was filled with water.

"The cup on my right leg contains water from heaven," the bird explained. "That on the left contains water from the nether world. Untie the cups now, and take care that no water is spilled from them."

So Benito untied the cups, taking great care with them. Thanking the bird, he was about to leave when the sparrow-hawk spoke once more.

"Tarry but a moment longer, Benito. In a moment I shall be dead, for I am weary unto death from my journey up into heaven and down into the nether world. My only request of you is that when I have died you will bury me."

In a very short time the bird was dead. Sad as it made him to do so, Benito buried the body of this faithful friend before he went on his way.

Upon returning to the palace, Benito delivered into the hands of the king the two cups of water which had been obtained at such sacrifice. The king took them without a word of gratitude to his servant who had served him so cheerfully and tirelessly.

When the waters were given to the princess by the king's own hands, she made one further request. She asked him to pour over her the water from heaven.

The king wondered at such a request, but he took the cup and poured heaven's waters over her. And lo! in an instant the lovely princess was transformed into the most beautiful woman that the sun had ever shone upon!

"Pour the waters over me!" the king demanded, for he wished to be as handsome as possible in order to equal this most beautiful of all creatures.

Taking the cup of water from the nether world, the princess poured it over the king, and immediately his body took the form of so ugly and horrible a spirit that no one could bear to look upon it. Fortunately for all, the sight soon vanished and the king was no more.

Now the princess turned to Benito, saying, "You, Benito, are the faithful one. You have been devoted to your parents, faithful to your master, kind to me in restoring my lost jewels, and brave in delivering me from the hands of the cruel giants. It is you whom I wish to have for my husband!"

Benito could hardly believe the good fortune that had come to him. Amid great rejoicing and feasting he and the princess were married. And as king and queen they ruled that kingdom well for all the remainder of their lives.

As for Benito's parents, he gave them everything their hearts desired, and more. And they and their son and his bride were so happy that the story of their happiness is still being told these many, many years after.

RETOLD BY ELIZABETH HOUGH SECHRIST

The Swineherd

There was once a poor prince who had only a tiny kingdom, but it was big enough to allow him to marry, and he was bent upon marrying.

Now it certainly was rather bold of him to say to the emperor's daughter, "Will you have me?" He did, however, venture to say so, for his name was known far and wide. And there were hundreds of princesses who would have said "Yes," and "Thank you, kindly," but see if *she* would!

Let us hear about it.

A rose tree grew on the grave of the prince's father. It was such a beautiful rose tree. But it bloomed only every fifth year, and then bore only one blossom. What a rose that was! By merely smelling it one forgot all of one's cares and sorrows.

Then he had a nightingale which sang as if every lovely melody in the world dwelt in her little throat. This rose and this nightingale were to be given to the princess, so they were put into great silver caskets and sent to her.

The emperor had them carried before him into the great hall where the princess was playing at "visiting" with her ladies-in-waiting—they had nothing else to do. When she saw the caskets with the gifts, she clapped her hands with delight.

"If it were only a little pussy cat!" said she. But there was the lovely rose.

"Oh, how exquisitely it is made!" said all the ladies-in-waiting.

"It is more than beautiful," said the emperor. "It is neatly made." But the princess touched it, and then she was ready to cry.

"Fie, Papa!" she said. "It is not made. It is a real one."

"Fie," said all the ladies-in-waiting. "It is a real one."

"Well, let us see what there is in the other casket, before we get angry," said the emperor, and out came the nightingale. It sang so beautifully that at first no one could find anything to say against it.

"Superbe! charmant!" said the ladies-in-waiting, for they all had a smattering of French; one spoke it worse than the other.

"How that bird reminds me of our lamented Empress' musical box," said an old courtier. "Ah yes, they are the same tunes and the same beautiful execution."

"So they are," said the emperor, crying like a little child.

"I should hardly think it could be a real one," said the princess.

"Yes, it is a real one," said those who had brought it.

"Oh, let that bird fly away, then," said the princess, and she would not hear of allowing the prince to come. But he was not to be crushed. He stained his face brown and black, and pressing his cap over his eyes, he knocked at the door.

"Good morning, Emperor," said he. "Can I be taken into service in the palace?"

"Well, there are so many wishing to do that," said the emperor. "But let me see. Yes, I need somebody to look after the pigs. We have so many of them."

So the prince was made imperial swineherd. A horrid little room was given him near the pigsties, and here he had to live. He sat busily at work all day, and by the evening he had made a beautiful little cooking pot. It had bells all round it, and when the pot boiled, they tinkled delightfully and played the old tune:

> *Ach du lieber Augustin,*
> *Alles ist weg, weg, weg!*

But the greatest of all its charms was that by holding one's finger in the steam, one could immediately smell all the dinners that were being cooked at every stove in the town. Now this was a very different matter from a rose.

The princess came walking along with all her ladies-in-waiting, and when she heard the tune she stopped and looked pleased, for she could play "Ach du lieber Augustin" herself. It was her only tune, and she could play it with only one finger.

"Why, that is my tune," she said. "This must be a cultivated swineherd. Ask him what the instrument costs."

So one of the ladies-in-waiting had to go into his room, but before she entered she put on wooden clog-shoes.

"How much do you want for the pot?" she asked.

"I must have ten kisses from the princess," said the swineherd.

"Heaven preserve us!" said the lady.

"I won't take less," said the swineherd.

"Well, what does he say?" asked the princess.

"I really cannot tell you," said the lady-in-waiting. "It is so shocking."

"Then you must whisper it." And she whispered it.

"He is a wretch!" said the princess, and went away at once. But she had gone only a little way when she heard the bells tinkling beautifully:

Ach du lieber Augustin . . .

"Go and ask him if he will take ten kisses from the ladies-in-waiting."

"No, thank you," said the swineherd. "Ten kisses from the princess, or I keep my pot."

"How tiresome it is," said the princess. "Then you will have to stand round me, so that no one may see."

So the ladies-in-waiting stood round her and spread out their skirts while the swineherd took his ten kisses, and then the pot was hers.

What a delight it was to them! The pot was kept on the boil day and night. They knew what was cooking on every stove in the town, from the chamberlain's to the shoemaker's. The ladies-in-waiting danced about and clapped their hands.

"We know who has sweet soup and pancakes for dinner, and who has cutlets. How amusing it is."

"Highly interesting," said the mistress of the robes.

"Yes, but hold your tongues, for I am the emperor's daughter."

"Heaven preserve us!" they all said.

The swineherd—that is to say the prince, only nobody knew that he was not a real swineherd—did not let the day pass in idleness, and he now constructed a rattle. When it was swung around it played all the waltzes, galops and jig tunes ever heard since the creation of the world.

"But this is *superbe!*" said the princess, as she walked by. "I have never heard finer compositions. Go and ask him what the instrument costs, but let us have no more kissing."

"He wants a hundred kisses from the princess," said the lady-in-waiting.

"I think he is mad!" said the princess, and she went away, but she had not gone far when she stopped.

"One must encourage art," she said. "I am the emperor's daughter. Tell him he can have ten kisses, the same as yesterday, and he can take the others from the ladies-in-waiting."

"But we don't like that at all," said the ladies.

"Oh, nonsense! If I can kiss him you can do the same. Remember that I pay you wages, as well as give you board and lodging." So the lady-in waiting had to go again.

"A hundred kisses from the princess, or let each keep his own."

"Stand in front of me," said she, and all the ladies stood round while he kissed her.

"Whatever is the meaning of that crowd round the pigsties?" said the emperor, as he stepped out onto the veranda. He rubbed his eyes and put on his spectacles. "Why, it is the ladies-in-waiting. What game are they up to? I must go and see!" So he pulled up the heels of his slippers, for they were shoes which he had trodden down.

Bless us, what a hurry he was in! When he got into the yard he walked very softly, and the ladies were so busy counting the kisses, so that there should be fair play, and neither too few nor too many kisses, that they never heard the emperor. He stood on tiptoe.

"What is all this?" he said when he saw what was going on, and he hit them on the head with his slipper just as the swineherd was taking his eighty-sixth kiss.

"Out you go!" said the emperor. He was furious, and he put both the princess and the prince out of his realm.

There she stood crying, and the swineherd scolded, and the rain poured down in torrents.

"Oh, miserable creature that I am!" said the princess. "If only

I had accepted the handsome prince. Oh, how unhappy I am!"

The swineherd went behind a tree, wiped the black and brown stain from his face, and threw away his ugly clothes. When he stepped out dressed as a prince, he was so handsome that the princess could not help curtseying to him.

"I am come to despise thee," he said. "Thou wouldst not have an honorable prince. Thou couldst not prize the rose or the nightingale. But thou wouldst kiss the swineherd for a trumpery musical box! As thou hast made thy bed, so must thou lie upon it."

Then he went back into his own little kingdom and shut and locked the door. So she had to stand outside and sing in earnest:

> *Ach du lieber Augustin,*
> *Alles ist weg, weg, weg!*

HANS CHRISTIAN ANDERSEN

The Shepherd's Nosegay

There was once a king who had a beautiful daughter. When it was time for her to get a husband, the king set a day and invited all the neighboring princes to come and see her.

One of these princes decided that he would like to have a look at the princess before the others. So, he dressed himself in a shepherd's costume: a broad-brimmed hat, a blue smock, a green vest, tight breeches to the knees, thick woolen stockings, and sandals. Thus disguised, he set out for the kingdom where the princess lived. All he took with him were four loaves of bread to eat on the way.

He hadn't gone far before he met a beggar who begged him, in God's name, for a piece of bread. The prince at once gave him one of the four loaves. A little farther on a second beggar held out his hand and begged for a piece of bread. To him the prince gave the second loaf. To a third beggar he gave the third loaf, and to a fourth beggar the last loaf.

The fourth beggar said to him, "Prince in shepherd's guise, your charity will not go unrewarded. Here are four gifts for you, one for each of the loaves of bread that you have given away this day. Take this whip, which has the power of killing anyone it strikes, however gentle the blow. Take this beggar's wallet. It has in it some bread and cheese, but not common bread and cheese, for, no matter how much of it you eat, there will always be some left. Take this shepherd's ax. If ever you have to leave your sheep alone, plant it in the earth and the sheep, instead of straying, will graze around it. Last, here is a shepherd's pipe. When you blow upon it, your sheep will dance and play. Farewell, and good luck go with you."

The prince thanked the beggar for his gifts and then trudged on to the kingdom where the beautiful princess lived. He presented himself at the palace as a shepherd in quest of work, and he told them his name was Yan. The king liked his appearance, and so the next day he was put in charge of a flock of sheep, which he drove up the mountainside to pasture.

He planted his shepherd's ax in the midst of a meadow and, leaving his sheep to graze about it, he went off into the forest hunting adventures. There he came upon a castle where a giant was busy cooking his dinner in a big saucepan.

"Good day to you," Yan said politely.

The giant, who was a rude, unmannerly fellow, bellowed out, "It won't take me long to finish you, you young whippersnapper!"

He raised a great iron club to strike Yan, but Yan, quick as thought, flicked the giant with his whip and the huge fellow toppled over dead.

The next day he returned to the castle and found another giant in possession.

"Ho, ho!" he roared on sight of Yan. "What, you young whippersnapper, back again! You killed my brother yesterday and now I'll kill you!"

He raised his great iron club to strike Yan, but Yan skipped nimbly aside. Then he flicked the giant with his whip, and the huge fellow toppled over dead.

When Yan returned to the castle the third day, there were no more giants about, so he wandered from room to room to see what treasures were there.

In one room he found a big chest. He struck it smartly, and immediately two burly men jumped out and, bowing low before him, said, "What does the master of the castle desire?"

"Show me everything there is to be seen," Yan ordered.

The two servants of the chest showed him everything—jewels and treasures and gold. Then they led him out into the gardens, where the most wonderful flowers in the world were blooming. Yan plucked some of these and made them into a nosegay.

That afternoon, as he drove home his sheep, he played on his magic pipe, and the sheep, pairing off two by two, began to dance and frisk about him. All the people in the village ran out to see the strange sight and laughed and clapped their hands for joy.

The princess ran to the palace window, and when she saw the sheep dancing two by two, she, too, laughed and clapped her hands. Then the wind whiffed her a smell of the wonderful nosegay that Yan was carrying, and she said to her serving maid, "Run down to the shepherd and tell him the Princess desires his nosegay."

The serving maid delivered the message to Yan, but he shook his head and said, "Tell your mistress that whoever wants this nosegay must come herself and say, 'Yanitchko, give me that nosegay.'"

When the princess heard this, she laughed and said, "What an odd shepherd! I see I must go myself."

So, the princess herself came out to Yan and said, "Yanitchko, give me that nosegay."

But Yan smiled and shook his head. "Whoever wants this nosegay must say, 'Yanitchko, please give me that nosegay.'"

The princess was a merry girl, so she laughed and said, "Yanitchko, please give me that nosegay."

Yan gave it to her at once and she thanked him sweetly.

The next day Yan went again to the castle garden and plucked another nosegay. Then in the afternoon he drove his sheep through the village as before, playing his pipe. The princess was standing at the palace window waiting to see him. When the wind brought her a whiff of the fresh nosegay that was even more fragrant than the first one, she ran out to Yan and said, "Yanitchko, please give me that nosegay."

But Yan smiled and shook his head. "Whoever wants this nosegay must say, 'My dear Yanitchko, I beg you most politely please to give me that nosegay.'"

"My dear Yanitchko," the princess repeated demurely, "I beg you most politely please to give me that nosegay."

So, Yan gave her the second nosegay. The princess put it in her window, and the fragrance filled the village until people came from far and near to see it.

After that, every day Yan gathered a nosegay for the princess, and every day the princess stood at the palace window waiting to see the handsome shepherd. And always when she asked for the nosegay she said "please."

In this way a month went by, and the day arrived when the neighboring princes were to come to meet the princess. They were to come in fine array, the people said, and the princess had ready a kerchief and a ring for the one who would please her most.

Yan planted the ax in the meadow and, leaving the sheep to graze about it, went to the castle, where he ordered the servants of the chest to dress him as befitted his rank. They put a white suit upon him and gave him a white horse with trappings of silver.

He rode to the palace and took his place with the other princes, but behind them, so that the princess had to crane her neck to see him.

One by one the various princes rode by the princess, but to none of them did the princess give her kerchief and ring. Yan was the last to salute her, and instantly she handed him her favors.

Then before the king or the other suitors could speak to him, Yan put spurs to his horse and rode off.

That evening when he was driving home his sheep as usual, the princess ran out to him and said, "Yan, it was you!"

But Yan laughed and put her off. "How can a poor shepherd be a prince?" he asked.

The princess was not convinced, and she said in another month, when the princes were to come again, she would find out.

For another month Yan tended sheep and plucked nosegays for the merry little princess, and the princess waited for him at the palace window every afternoon, and when she saw him, she always spoke to him politely and said "please."

When the day for the second meeting of the princes came, the servants of the chest arrayed Yan in a suit of red and gave him a sorrel horse with trappings of gold. Yan again rode to the palace and took his place with the other princes, but behind them, so that the princess had to crane her neck to see him.

Again the suitors rode by the princess one by one, but at each of them she shook her head impatiently and kept her kerchief and ring until Yan saluted her.

Instantly the ceremony was over, Yan put spurs to his horse and rode off, and although the king sent after him to bring him back, Yan was able to escape.

That evening when he was driving home his sheep, the princess ran out to him and said, "Yanitchko, it was you! I know it was!"

But again Yan laughed and put her off and asked her how she could think such a thing of a poor shepherd.

Again the princess was not convinced, and she said in another month, when the princes were to come for the third and last time, she would make sure.

For another month Yan tended his sheep and plucked nose-gays for the merry little princess, and the princess waited for him at the palace window every afternoon, and when she saw him, she always said politely, "please."

For the third meeting of the princes the servants of the chest arrayed Yan in a gorgeous suit of black and gave him a black horse with golden trappings studded in diamonds. He rode to the palace and took his place behind the other suitors. Things went as before, and again the princess saved her kerchief and ring for him.

This time, when he tried to ride off, the other suitors surrounded him, and before he escaped, one of them wounded him on the foot.

He galloped back to the castle in the forest, dressed once again in his shepherd's clothes, and returned to the meadow where his sheep were grazing. There he sat down and bound up his wounded foot in the kerchief that the princess had given him. Then, when he had eaten some bread and cheese from his magic wallet, he stretched himself out in the sun and fell asleep.

Meanwhile, the princess, who was sorely vexed that her mysterious suitor had again escaped, slipped out of the palace and ran up the mountain path to see for herself whether the shepherd was really with his sheep. She found Yan asleep, and when she saw her kerchief bound about his foot, she knew that he was the prince.

She woke him up and cried, "You are he! You know you are!"

Yan looked at her and laughed and he asked, "How can I be a prince?"

"But I know you are!" the princess said. "Oh, Yanitchko, dear Yanitchko, I beg you please to tell me!"

Then Yan, because he always did anything the princess asked him when she said "please," told her his true name and his rank.

The princess, overjoyed to hear that her dear shepherd was really a prince, carried him off to her father, the king.

"This is the man I shall marry," she said; "this and none other."

So Yan and the merry little princess were married and lived very happily. And the people of the country, when they speak of the princess, always say, "That's a princess for you! Why, even if she is a princess, she always says 'please' to her own husband!"

RETOLD BY PARKER FILLMORE

Rags-and-Tatters

A king, lying on his deathbed, called his only son to him, and said, "Dear Son, you shall be King after me. Your three sisters have no one but you to protect them. Be kind to them; but when it is time for them to marry, do not go about asking all the great princes of the earth to be their husbands. You know the rose tree that grows in the palace garden and flowers all the year round. Pluck a rose from it, throw it into the street, and whoever shall pick it up shall have your eldest sister for his wife. So for the second. So for the third."

It was the last wish of the dying king, and his son could not disobey. Therefore, when the eldest sister had grown up into a beautiful princess and the ministers said it was time for her to marry, her brother told her of their father's command.

"Oh, I'd rather not marry at all!" she said.

But the ministers said she must. So one day the young king plucked the rose, threw it into the street, and told the sentry at the palace door to watch who should pick it up, and send him into the royal presence. Soon there came walking along a fine young count, splendidly dressed, with a jeweled sword by his side, and brave and jolly of mien. He saw the rose, picked it up and stuck it in his velvet cap.

"The king demands to speak with you," said the sentry, stepping foward.

The count desired nothing better. He entered the palace, and presented himself before the king, who said to him, "You have been chosen as the husband of my eldest sister." The count bowed low, delighted at the honor.

But the princess grumbled, "I should have married a king, or a king's son at the least!" Her brother, however, had given his word; and in time she thought to herself, "Well, at least he is young and handsome and brave and gay. I might have fared much worse." And so she married the count.

A little later it was time for the second princess to marry. She was just as unwilling as her elder sister to take the first-comer; but her brother silenced her complaints, saying, "Such was our father's command!" So he plucked a rose, threw it out in the street, and bade the sentry watch who should pick it up. By and by a rich merchant came along, a grave, serious, solid and dignified person. He saw the rose, looked at it as if it were a pity it should be wasted, picked it up, and stopped to place it neatly in the buttonhole of his fine cloth doublet.

"The king desires to speak with you," said the sentry, stepping forward.

"It is a great honor," replied the citizen. "I will attend His Majesty without delay." And he entered the palace and heard what the king had to say to him. "I am not even noble," replied the citizen. "The princess might surely marry a much greater man than I."

"It was her father's wish," said the king; and the matter was settled.

The princess grumbled at first. A mere merchant, indeed! "But at least he is rich and honest and not at all ill-looking. I might have fared worse." So she married the merchant and went to her new home.

At last came the turn of Julietta, the youngest. For her the king did as for the others. He plucked the rose, threw it into the street, and told the sentry to watch who should pick it up, and send him in. Now, who should come by but a poor lame water carrier! Such an ugly, dirty little man! He saw the rose, picked it up, and put it to his lips.

"Now things are getting into a mess!" thought the sentry. But he dared not disobey the king's command, and stepping forward, he said to the water carrier, "The king desires to speak with you."

The poor man shrank back and looked at his tattered clothes

and ragged sandals. But when the king commands. . . He slunk up the marble steps and entered the palace.

"You picked up the rose?" said the king, eyeing him with dismay.

"Yes, sire! I meant no harm."

"Then you must marry my youngest sister, Julietta."

"Your Majesty is pleased to make a mock of me."

"Not at all! Not at all!" And he told of the dead king's command.

"But I am miserably poor, as you see—and lame of a leg—and ugly! It is impossible!"

"I wish it were!" replied the king. "But I have given my word."

"Then let her know who she's going to marry, a poor wretch who can scarcely feed her! And if it must be, don't send any dowry with her. I want no fine wife."

The grief of the poor young princess was heartrending. Her brother wept too, and it was a miserable wedding. But it couldn't be helped. So Julietta went away with her water carrier to his mean hut on the hill; and on the way all the people who saw them cried, "Look! there goes the princess with old Rags-and-Tatters!" Home she went to the miserable place, to live there with Rags-and-Tatters and his old crone of a mother.

"This is no place for fine clothes," said the old woman. She gave her a rough dress to wear, and wooden shoes, and made her scour and wash and bake and darn, and tend her husband's lame leg. There was only the coarsest food to eat—and little enough of that either.

Julietta wept and wept, and would not be comforted. Now, Rags-and-Tatters, though he did not want so fine a wife, was a kindhearted man, and he was full of pity for her. But what could he do? The only time she had any joy was when she was asleep, for then she dreamt beautiful dreams. One night she dreamt she was in a grand palace, warm and light and spacious. There were people all round to serve her, or to sing and play to her. She wore lovely clothes and jewels in her hair; and the tables were spread with things good to eat. She sat down to table with friends as beautiful as herself; and everyone was gay. When she woke up she told her husband all about it. But Rags-and-Tatters only said, "Dreams! Dreams! Think no more about it. It's time to get up and kindle the fire."

But next night she was in the beautiful palace again. And there was no waking up in the morning in her miserable hut on the hillside. No, she was in a lovely bedchamber, and maidens were arraying her in dainty garments. And when she went into another room, servants brought her breakfast and waited for her orders.

"I want a carriage," she said. Instantly a great gold coach and white horses stood before the door. She got in, and bade the coachman drive to her brother's palace. There she invited the young king and his wife to a banquet.

They accepted, but with amazement. They rode back with her, still wondering. "Has your husband then grown so rich?" they asked at last. But she would say nothing of her husband. On their way they drove to her sisters' houses, and brought them, their husbands, and other old friends besides, on to the feast.

Everything was ready for them. They ate, drank, and made merry, and musicians made music loud and soft. But ere the feast had ended one of them looked up to the gold ceiling. Now, there was a hole in the ceiling, and in the hole sat Rags-and-Tatters, looking down on them all with a grin on his face.

"Why, there is Rags-and-Tatters!" said the guest.

Then, in the winking of an eye, guests, feast, lights, music, palace, all disappeared, and the Princess Julietta was sitting by her hearth in the miserable hut on the hillside.

That evening when her husband came home she told him what had befallen her. He only laughed and said, "Dreams! Dreams! Think no more about it." And she had to take his old coat and mend it, for it was nearly falling to pieces.

Some weeks later she dreamt the same dream again, and, of course, she told her husband about it in the morning. "Oh, you with your dreams!" he said. "They're all nonsense! This is washing-day. Over the washing-tub you'll forget them." But the water in the tub was salt with her tears.

And that very night back she was in the beautiful palace, with servants to wait on her, and jeweled clothes to wear. When she called for a coach, the gold coach and the white horses were again at the door, and again she rode off in it to invite her brother and sisters, her kinsfolk and friends to a banquet. Again the banquet was rich and splendid, the flowers were rare and fragrant, and the music gay and soft, just as before. But as they were rising from the table someone looked up at the golden ceiling, and there in the hole the little man was sitting, grinning down at them all. "Look! look! There is Rags-and-Tatters!" he cried. And in the twinkling of an eye everything vanished, and the princess was back by her hearth in the hut on the hill, clad in her old frock, and darning her mother-in-law's rough stockings.

When her husband came home she moaned to him over all she had lost. In his heart he was really very sorry for her, but he only laughed. "Dreams! Dreams!" he said. "You dream sleeping.

You dream waking. Now, is my supper ready? I am hungry as a hawk."

For weeks and weeks she wept every day, and then one night she dreamt once more of the beautiful palace, and told her husband about it in the morning. But he only laughed.

Next night, however, she was back in the lovely palace again, richly clad, and with servants to wait on her. "Call my coach!" she cried. The gold coach and the white horses were at the door on the instant. Off she rode, invited all her kith and kin, her old friends and neighbors, to a banquet, and brought them back with her. The banquet was more splendid than ever. But before they sat down the Princess Julietta spoke to her assembled guests. "Make merry, my friends," she said. "Treat my house as your own. Only one thing is forbidden. Let none of you breathe the name of Rags-and-Tatters!"

They all sat down, ate, drank and made merry, and delicious music sounded all about them the while. Then one of the company looked up at the hole in the golden roof, and there he spied the little man grinning down on them all. It was just on the tip of his tongue to cry "Rags-and-Tatters," but he caught himself in time. And the princess herself looked up and saw the figure in the hole in the roof. A sudden ray of pity lit up her heart. "Poor man!" she said to herself. "What a good fellow he is, and how I sadden him with my complaints! I wish he were down here with us in the midst of it all, and enjoying it too!"

And then—did the lights, the music, the flowers and the guests, the palace and all, disappear as before? Not at all! The guests and their hostess rose from table, and entered another great hall, at the end of which stood two thrones of gold. On one of them sat a fair young prince, clad in velvet and jewels. His hair shone like the sun, and his eyes were of hyacinth blue, and his smile gladdened the heart of everyone. While they stood in amazement, he rose and said, "Welcome, my guests! My wife has entertained you while I have been on a journey. You will not be less merry, I hope, now that I have come home!" And he drew the Princess Julietta forward and placed her on the throne by the side of his own. Then they danced and sang and were joyous till the stars faded and daylight streamed through the windows of the hall.

For Rags-and-Tatters was not Rags-and-Tatters at all, but Prince Florio, the son of the King of Portugal! A wicked enchantress had cast on him a spell, because his father had banished her from his lands. The spell was to last till he should be loved by a princess whom he had brought to poverty. Now Julietta had broken it when she pitied and loved and longed for him in the midst of her splendor, rags and tatters and all.

But what of his old mother? She was not his mother, of course, but the wicked enchantress herself, who had delighted in watching the misery of the spellbound prince and his wife, and had made him believe he was really her son and doomed from his birth to hunger and rags.

Prince Florio and Princess Julietta went home to Portugal, and there they lived long and gloriously. But the castle where were held the enchanted banquets was never seen any more.

There's my story. It isn't very long.
If it isn't worth a penny, it's maybe worth a song.

ANNE MACDONNELL

The Sack of Truth

It makes many years in Spain since there was a King who had only one daughter. Since the Infanta was born she had been sickly. Years passed. As she grew older she grew no better; the royal doctors could find no cure for her malady.

"If the doctors of Spain are know-nothings, we will send for those of other countries," said the King.

That brought doctors from everywhere, and only one of them could mention a cure. He was a small Arabian doctor and he said: "Send for the finest pears in Spain. Enough of them will cure her."

So the King ordered pears—baskets of them. Whoever should bring in the best ones and cure the Infanta should have the wish of his heart granted. The King swore it by the good Santiago, patron saint of all Spain.

Many came, bringing good pears and bad pears, yellow and green pears, juicy and withered pears; and the Infanta would eat none of them.

Outside a small village there lived a peasant with three sons. Close to their hut grew a pear tree that every summer was covered with heart-shaped, fragrant pears, the color of gold.

One day the peasant said to the oldest son: "Take a basket, fill it with pears, take it to the King's palace and see can you not cure the Infanta."

The oldest set out with his basket, covered to keep the insects off. On the road he came up with a sad-faced woman carrying a little child. She stopped him and asked: "Boy, where are you going?"

"That isn't your business."

"What does your basket hold?"

"Horns!"

"Then let them be horns!"

Sure enough. When the oldest son reached the palace and un-covered his basket, it was filled with horns. So angry was the King that he ordered him thrown into the dungeon.

After a bit, when the oldest son did not return, the peasant said to the second son: "Something has happened to your brother. Go you, fill a basket with pears and try your luck."

The second son set out. On the road he came up with the sad-faced woman carrying the little child. She stopped him and asked: "Boy, where are you going?"

"That isn't your business."

"What does your basket hold?"

"Stones."

"Then let them be stones!"

Sure enough. When the second son reached the palace and uncovered his basket, it was filled with stones. If the King had been angry before, now he was purple and bursting. He ordered the second son thrown into the dungeon with his brother.

After a bit, when neither son returned, the peasant caught the youngest, whose name was Pedro, filling a basket under the pear tree. He was sad, frightened. "What are you doing? You cannot go. How shall I run the farm with no sons? Why should you be thinking that the youngest will succeed where the oldest has failed?"

The youngest shook his head. No one had ever thought him very clever, only kind and willing and cheerful. "There is the old saying, you know," he said at last—" 'The fingers of one hand are never equal.' I may find luck where my brothers missed it."

So Pedro set out with his basket of pears. On the road he came up with the sad-faced woman carrying a little child. She stopped him and asked: "Boy, where are you going?"

"Mother, I am going to the King's palace."

"What does your basket hold?"

Pears, to cure the Infanta of her long sickness."

And he thought to himself: "I must not be greedy with those pears. There is the old saying—'He who plays the fox for a day, pays for a year.' " So he uncovered the basket quickly, took out a pear and held it toward the child, saying: "*Nene,* would you like it? It is for you."

The woman took it for the child, smiling, and said: "Then let them be pears to cure! And for the one you have given away, ask what you will in return."

Pedro thought hard. "I would like a whistle which will call to me any animal I choose when I blow it."

"Here it is," said the woman, and she drew out of her kerchief a silver whistle strung on a cord so that Pedro could hang it around his neck.

When he arrived at the palace and uncovered his basket before the King, there were the pears, heart-shaped, fragrant, the color of gold. The King was overcome with joy when he saw them. "They are the best pears in the world!" he cried. "We will take them to the Infanta and see will she eat one."

The Infanta ate one—two—three. She would have eaten them

all if the court doctor would have let her. Already there was a faint health showing in her cheeks.

"What do you want?" asked the King.

"My brothers."

The King had them released. Pedro was grateful. He thought of the old saying: "Gratitude is better scattered than kept in one's pocket." So he climbed the nearest mountain, blew on his whistle

and called to him a wild hare. This he carried to the King. "Mark him; he is yours. Then free him. When I come back I will call him to you again. It shall be a sign between us of two men of honor."

But the King was astonished. "That is beyond your power to call back a wild hare. Nevertheless, if you do it, you shall marry the Infanta."

Over the world went Pedro with his silver whistle; calling to him creatures of all kinds, great and small, fierce and gentle. These he used in good service to others, and you can see how that might be.

At the end of a year he returned to Spain and the King's palace. But while he was still a long way off he blew for the hare and it came running to him, the King's mark still on it. The King saw them approaching from the balcony, the hare under Pedro's arm. He called for his prime minister. "There is that boy back again and with him the wild hare. You must bargain the creature away or I shall have to let him marry the Infanta."

Pedro sold the hare to the minister for a pound of gold. And when he had gone he whistled the hare back to him.

From his balcony the King watched. He saw what had happened. He was frantic—frantic. He called the underminister. "Go bargain for that hare; and after you have paid for it, see that you don't lose it as the prime minister did. Hurry, hurry."

The underminister had to pay two pounds of gold for the hare; and before he had reached the palace gates with it, Pedro had whistled it back again. "This is terrible—terrible!" said the King when he saw what had happened. This time he sent the Infanta, who returned saying that Pedro would only bargain with the King.

So the King went. Pedro drew him into the shadow of a plane tree. "You may have the hare for nothing, Your Majesty, if— you will kiss him."

The King was outraged. But what could he do? "Look carefully about. Is there anyone looking?" he asked.

"No one."

The King kissed the hare, just where Pedro's finger pointed. He followed the King back to the palace. Inside, in the Hall of Justice, before the entire court, Pedro asked: "You will keep your promise, yes? I marry the Infanta?"

But the King did not want that. Who ever heard of an Infanta of Spain marrying the son of a peasant? It was abominable. He must think a way out. The prime minister thought of it and whispered in the King's ear: "Tell him he must take a sack, travel the world over and fill it with truth."

The King told Pedro what he must do first if he was to marry the Infanta.

"Good. Fetch me a sack."

The King sent for a large sack.

Pedro took it. He opened the mouth of it until it gaped wide. He said: "I have no need to travel to find truth enough to fill it. King, answer me: Is it not the truth that I brought a basket of the best pears to the palace?"

"It is."

"Truth, go into the sack," and he made a motion as if flinging it inside. "King, is it not the truth that those pears cured the Infanta?"

"It is."

"Truth, go into the sack. King, is it not true that I gave the wild hare to you as a sign between us of two men of honor?"

"It is."

"Truth, go into the sack. King, is it not the truth that you put your mark upon that hare, freed it; and that I brought it back to you again?"

"It is."

"Truth, go into the sack. King, is it not the truth that in order to escape your promise and get the hare from me you kissed . . ."

"Stop!" said the King. "The sack is full of truth."

"And I marry the Infanta?"

"Agreed."

In a day they were married; in a year they had a son; in another year, a daughter. But it took a lifetime for them to get to the end of their happiness.

RUTH SAWYER

The Nightingale

In China, as you know, the emperor is a Chinaman, and all the people around him are Chinamen too. It is many years since the story I am going to tell you happened, but that is all the more reason for telling it, lest it should be forgotten.

The emperor's palace was the most beautiful thing in the world. It was made entirely of finest porcelain, which was very costly, and so fragile that it could be touched only with the very greatest of care. The most extraordinary flowers were to be seen in the garden. The most beautiful ones had little silver bells tied to them which tinkled perpetually, so that no one could pass the flowers without looking at them. Every little detail in the garden had been most carefully thought out, and it was so big that even the gardener himself did not know where it ended.

If one went on walking, one came to beautiful woods with lofty trees and deep lakes. The wood extended to the sea, which was deep and blue, deep enough for large ships to sail up right under the branches of the trees. Among these trees lived a nightingale, which sang so deliciously that even the poor fisherman, who had plenty of other things to do, lay still to listen to it when he was out at night drawing in his nets.

"Heavens, how beautiful it is!" he said, but then he had to attend to his business and forgot it. The next night when he heard it again he would again exclaim, "Heavens, how beautiful it is!"

Travelers came to the emperor's capital from every country in the world. They admired everything very much, especially the palace and the gardens, but when they heard the nightingale they all said, "This is better than anything."

When they got home they described it, and learned men wrote many books about the town, the palace, and the garden. But nobody forgot the nightingale—it was always put above everything else. Those among them who were poets wrote the most beautiful poems, all about the nightingale in the woods by the deep blue sea. These books went all over the world, and in course of time some of them reached the emperor. He sat in his golden chair reading and reading, and nodding his head, well pleased to hear such beautiful descriptions of the town, the palace, and the garden. "But the nightingale is the best of all," he read.

"What is this?" said the emperor. "The nightingale? Why, I know nothing about it. Is there such a bird in my kingdom, and in my own garden, and I have never heard of it? Imagine my having to discover this from a book."

Then he called his gentleman-in-waiting, who was so grand that when anyone of a lower rank dared to speak to him or to ask him a question, he would only answer, "P," which means nothing at all.

"There is said to be a very wonderful bird called a nightingale here," said the emperor. "They say that it is better than anything else in all my great kingdom. Why have I never been told anything about it?"

"I have never heard it mentioned," said the gentleman-in-waiting. "It has never been presented at court."

"I wish it to appear here this evening to sing to me," said the emperor. "The whole world knows what I am possessed of, and I know nothing about it!"

"I have never heard it mentioned before," said the gentleman-in-waiting. "I will seek it, and I will find it."

But where was it to be found? The gentleman-in-waiting ran upstairs and downstairs and in and out of all the rooms and corridors. No one of all those he met had ever heard anything about the nightingale. So the gentleman-in-waiting ran back to the emperor and said that it must be a myth, invented by the writers of the books. "Your Imperial Majesty must not believe everything that is written! Books are often mere inventions, even if they do not belong to what we call the black art."

"But the book in which I read it was sent to me by the powerful Emperor of Japan. Therefore it can't be untrue. I will hear this nightingale. I insist upon its being here tonight. I extend my most gracious protection to it, and if it is not forthcoming, I will have the whole court trampled upon after supper."

"Tsing-pe!" said the gentleman-in-waiting, and away he ran again, up and down all the stairs, in and out of all the rooms and corridors. Half the court ran with him, for none of them wished to be trampled on. There was much questioning about this nightingale, which was known to all the outside world but to no one at court.

At last they found a poor little maid in the kitchen, who said, "Oh heavens! The nightingale? I know it very well. Yes indeed, it can sing. Every evening I am allowed to take broken meat to my poor sick mother, who lives down by the shore. On my way back, when I am tired I rest awhile in the wood, and then I hear the nightingale. Its song brings the tears into my eyes. I feel as if my mother were kissing me."

"Little kitchen maid," said the gentleman-in-waiting, "I will procure you a permanent position in the kitchen and permission to see the Emperor dining if you will take us to the nightingale. It is commanded to appear at court tonight."

Then they all went out into the wood where the nightingale usually sang. Half the court was there. As they were going along at their best pace, a cow began to bellow.

"Oh," said a young courtier, "there we have it. What wonderful power for such a little creature. I have certainly heard it before."

"No, those are the cows bellowing. We are a long way from the place." Then frogs began to croak in the marsh.

"How beautiful!" said the Chinese chaplain. "It is just like the tinkling of church bells."

"No, those are the frogs," said the little kitchen maid. "But I think we shall soon hear it now."

Then the nightingale began to sing.

"Listen, listen! There it sits," said the little girl. And she pointed to a little gray bird up among the branches.

"Is it possible," said the gentleman-in-waiting. "I should never have thought it was like that. How common it looks. Seeing so many grand people must have frightened all its colors away."

"Little nightingale," called the kitchen maid quite loud, "Our Gracious Emperor wishes you to sing to him."

"With the greatest pleasure," said the nightingale, warbling away in most delightful fashion.

"It is just like crystal bells," said the gentleman-in-waiting. "Look at its little throat, how active it is. It is extraordinary that we have never heard it before. I am sure it will be a great success at court."

"Shall I sing again to the Emperor?" said the nightingale, who thought he was present.

"My precious little nightingale," said the gentleman-in-waiting, "I have the honor to command your attendance at a court festival tonight, where you will charm His Gracious Majesty the Emperor with your fascinating singing."

"It sounds best among the trees," said the nightingale, but it went with them willingly when it heard that the emperor wished it.

The palace had been brightened up for the occasion. The walls and the floors, which were all of china, shone by the light of many thousand golden lamps. The most beautiful flowers, all of the tinkling kind, were arranged in the corridors. There was hurrying to and fro, and a great draught, but this was just what made the bells ring. One's ears were full of the tinkling. In the middle of the large reception room where the emperor sat, a golden rod had been fixed, on which the nightingale was to perch. The whole court was assembled, and the little kitchen maid had been permitted to stand behind the door, as she now had the actual title of Cook. They were all dressed in their best. Everybody's eyes were turned toward the little gray bird at which the emperor was nodding.

The nightingale sang delightfully, and the tears came into the emperor's eyes and rolled down his cheeks. And when the nightingale sang more beautifully than ever, its notes melted all hearts. The emperor was so charmed that he said the nightingale should have his gold slipper to wear round its neck. But the nightingale declined with thanks—it had already been sufficiently rewarded.

"I have seen tears in the eyes of the Emperor," he said. "That is my richest reward. The tears of an Emperor have a wonderful power. God knows I am sufficiently recompensed." And it again burst into its sweet, heavenly song.

"That is the most delightful coquetting I have ever seen!" said the ladies. And they took some water into their mouths to try and make the same gurgling, when anyone spoke to them, thinking so to equal the nightingale. Even the lackeys and the chambermaids

announced that they were satisfied, and that is saying a great deal. They are always the most difficult people to please. Yes indeed, the nightingale had made a sensation. It was to stay at court now, and have its own cage, as well as liberty to walk out twice a day and once in the night. It always had twelve footmen, with each one holding a ribbon which was tied round its leg. There was not much pleasure in an outing of that sort.

The whole town talked about the marvelous bird. If two people met, one said to the other "Night," and the other answered "Gale." And then they sighed, perfectly understanding each other. Eleven cheesemongers' children were named after it, but not one among them could sing anything.

One day a large parcel came for the emperor. Outside was written the word "Nightingale."

"Here we have another new book about this celebrated bird," said the emperor. But it was not a book. It was a little work of art in a box, an artificial nightingale exactly like the living one, except that it was studded all over with diamonds, rubies, and sapphires.

When the artificial bird was wound up, it could sing one of the songs the real one sang, and it wagged its tail, which glittered with silver and gold. A ribbon was tied round its neck on which was written, "The Emperor of Japan's nightingale is very poor compared to the Emperor of China's."

Everybody said, "Oh, how beautiful!" And the person who brought the artificial bird immediately received the title of Imperial Nightingale-Carrier-in-Chief.

"Now, they must sing together. What a duet that will be!"

Then they had to sing together, but they did not get on very well, for the real nightingale sang in its own way and the artificial one could only sing waltzes.

"There is no fault in that," said the music master. "It is perfectly in time and correct in every way."

Then the artificial bird had to sing alone. It was just as great a success as the real one, and it was much prettier to look at, because it glittered like bracelets and breastpins.

It sang the same tune three and thirty times over, and yet it was not tired. People would willingly have heard it from the beginning again, but the emperor said that the real one must have a turn now. But where was it? No one had noticed that it had flown out of the open window, back to its own green woods.

"What is the meaning of this?" said the emperor.

All the courtiers railed at it and said it was a most ungrateful bird.

"We have got the best bird, though," said they, and then the artificial bird had to sing again. This was the thirty-fourth time that they had heard the same tune, but they did not know it thoroughly even yet because it was so difficult.

The music master praised the bird tremendously and insisted that it was better than the real nightingale, not only on the outside, with all its diamonds, but inside too.

"You see, my ladies and gentlemen, and the Emperor before all, in the real nightingale you never know what you will hear, but in the artificial one everything is decided beforehand. So it is, and so it must remain. It can't be otherwise. You can account for things: you can open it and show the human ingenuity in arranging how the waltzes go, and how one note follows upon another."

"Those are exactly my opinions," they all said, and the music master got leave to show the bird to the public next Sunday. They were also to hear it sing, said the emperor. So they heard it, and all became as enthusiastic over it as if they had drunk themselves merry on tea, because that is a thoroughly Chinese habit.

Then they all said, "Oh!" and stuck their forefingers in the air and nodded their heads.

But the poor fisherman who had heard the real nightingale said, "It sounds very nice, and it is very nearly like the real one, but there is something wanting. I don't know what." The real nightingale was banished from the kingdom.

The artificial bird had its place on a silken cushion, close to the emperor's bed. All the presents it had received of gold and precious jewels were scattered round it. Its title had risen to be Chief Imperial Singer-of-the-Bedchamber. In rank it stood number one on the left side, for the emperor reckoned that side where the heart was seated was the important one. And even an emperor's heart is on the left side.

The music master wrote five and twenty volumes about the artificial bird. The treatise was very long, and was written in all the most difficult Chinese characters. Everybody said they had read and understood it, for otherwise they would have been reckoned stupid, and then their bodies would have been trampled upon.

Things went on in this way for a whole year. The emperor, the court, and all the other Chinamen knew every little gurgle in the song of the artificial bird by heart. But they liked it all the better for this, and they could all join in the song themselves. Even the street boys sang "Zizizi! cluck, cluck, cluck!" And the emperor sang it too.

But one evening, when the bird was singing its best and the emperor was lying in bed listening to it, something gave way inside the bird with a *whizz*. *Whirr!* went all the wheels, and the music stopped.

The emperor jumped out of bed and sent for his private physicians, but what good could they do? Then they sent for the watchmaker, who after a good deal of talk and examination got the works to go again somehow. But he said the bird would have to be spared as much as possible, because it was so worn out, and that he could not renew the works so as to be sure of the tune. This was a great blow! They now dared to let the artificial bird sing only once a year, and hardly that. But then the music master made a little speech using all the most difficult Chinese words. He said it was just as good as ever, and his saying it made it so.

Five years passed, and then a great grief came upon the nation. They were all very fond of their emperor, and now he was ill and could not live, it was said. A new emperor was already chosen, and people stood about in the street and asked the gentleman-in-waiting how the emperor was getting on.

"P," answered he, shaking his head.

The emperor lay pale and cold in his gorgeous bed. The courtiers thought he was dead, and they all went off to pay their respects to their new emperor. The lackeys ran off to talk matters over, and the chambermaids gave a great coffee party. Cloth had been laid down in all the rooms and corridors so as to deaden the sounds of footsteps, so it was very, very quiet. But the emperor was not dead yet. He lay stiff and pale in the gorgeous bed with velvet hangings and heavy golden tassels. There was an open window high above him, and the moon streamed in upon the emperor and the artificial bird beside him.

The poor emperor could hardly breathe. He seemed to have a weight on his chest. He opened his eyes and then he saw that it was Death sitting upon his chest, wearing his golden crown. In one hand he held the emperor's golden sword, and in the other his imperial banner. From among the folds of the velvet hangings peered many curious faces. Some were hideous, others gentle and pleasant. They were all the emperor's good and bad deeds, which now looked him in the face when Death was weighing him down.

"Do you remember that?" whispered one after the other. "Do you remember this?" And they told him so many things that the perspiration poured down his face.

"I never knew that," said the emperor. "Music, music! Sound the great Chinese drums," he cried, "that I may not hear what they are saying." But they went on and on, and Death sat nodding his head like a Chinaman at everything that was said. "Music, music!" shrieked the emperor. "You precious little golden bird, sing, sing! I have loaded you with precious stones, and even hung my own golden slipper round your neck. Sing, I tell you, sing!"

But the bird stood silent. There was nobody to wind it up, so of course it could not go. Death continued to fix the great empty sockets of its eyes upon him, and all was silent, terribly silent.

Suddenly, close to the window there was a burst of lovely song. It was the living nightingale, perched on a branch outside. It had heard of the emperor's need and had come to bring comfort and hope to him. As it sang, the faces round became fainter and fainter, and the blood coursed with fresh vigor in the emperor's veins and through his feeble limbs. Even Death himself listened to the song and said, "Go on, little nightingale, go on!"

"Yes, if you give me the gorgeous golden sword. Yes, if you give me the Imperial banner. Yes, if you give me the Emperor's crown."

And Death gave back each of these treasures for a song, and the nightingale went on singing. It sang about the quiet churchyard where the roses bloom, where the elder flowers scent the air, and where the fresh grass is ever moistened anew by the tears of the mourners. This song brought to Death a longing for his own garden, and like a cold gray mist he passed out of the window.

"Thanks, thanks!" said the emperor. "You heavenly little

bird, I know you. I banished you from my kingdom, and yet you have charmed the evil visions away from my bed by your song, and even Death away from my heart. How can I ever repay you?"

"You have rewarded me," said the nightingale. "I brought tears to your eyes the very first time I ever sang to you, and I shall never forget it. Those are the jewels which gladden the heart of a singer. But sleep now, and wake up fresh and strong. I will sing to you."

Then it sang again, and the emperor fell into a sweet, refreshing sleep. The sun shone in at his window, and he awoke refreshed and well. None of his attendants had yet come back to him, for they thought he was dead, but the nightingale still sat there singing.

"You must always stay with me," said the emperor. "You shall sing only when you like, and I will break the artificial bird into a thousand pieces."

"Don't do that," said the nightingale. "It did all the good it could. Keep it as you have always done. I can't build my nest and live in this palace, but let me come whenever I like. Then I will sit on the branch in the evening and sing to you. I will sing to cheer you and to make you thoughtful too. I will sing to you of the happy ones and of those that suffer. I will sing about the good and the evil, which are kept hidden from you. The little singing bird flies far and wide, to the poor fisherman and to the peasant's home, to numbers who are far from you and your court. I love your heart more than your crown, and yet there is an odor of sanctity round the crown too! I will come, and I will sing to you. But you must promise me one thing."

"Everything!" said the emperor, who stood there in his imperial robes, which he had just put on, and he held the sword heavy with gold upon his heart.

"Only one thing I ask you. Tell no one that you have a little bird who tells you everything. It will be better so."

Then the nightingale flew away. The attendants came in to look after their dead emperor—and there he stood, bidding them "Good morning!"

HANS CHRISTIAN ANDERSEN